D1429222

SCOTTISH
SHORT STORIES

SCOTTISH
SHORT STORIES
1978

Preface by Hugh Rae

COLLINS
St James's Place, London

William Collins Sons & Co Ltd
London · Glasgow · Sydney · Auckland
Toronto · Johannesburg

First published 1978

Published with the support of the Scottish Arts Council

ISBN 0 00 221889 5

Set in Monotype Imprint
Made and Printed in Great Britain by
William Collins Sons & Co Ltd Glasgow

CONTENTS

PREFACE

Selecting a handful of stories for publication from more than two hundred submissions is no easy task. No single entry proved to be outstanding. The overall standard, however, was exceedingly high and the editors of this sixth annual volume of Scottish Short Stories (Finlay J. Macdonald, Philip Ziegler and I) were mercifully spared the necessity of padding out the anthology from the best of a bad lot. Indeed, our only regret was that we were unable to publish all the stories that appealed to us.

There is nothing cabalistic in the art of editing. On the contrary, our primary response to the individual entries was entirely subjective. Did we, as readers, like the piece? Did the writer sing our kind of song? Significantly we found ourselves in almost immediate agreement over the majority of the stories that follow, proof that each fulfils the principal aim of the short story writer and communicates thoughts and emotions coherently and lucidly, a sharing of experience.

Variety happened by chance, the result of the diversity of interests of the current crop of writers rather than an imposed editorial contrivance. Our only collective criterion was that the story should be good of its kind.

Looking back over the entries in general, it is now possible to identify and localize certain motifs and, without stretching conclusions like a dreary academic, predict that the kailyard reminiscence is now losing its grip on the imagination. Hints and glimmers of the best qualities of the school remain in sharp characterization, excellence of atmosphere and a wry humour that is inimitably Scottish, all strong suits in this collection. The family, and its irrefragable demands on the psyche, is still a potent source of 'plot'; nation and family, in a small country, being locked at the interface of past and present.

Many of the titles themselves are a give-away, reflecting this almost obsessive concern with affectionate but troubled relationships, the internecine warfare between home, family, nation and the niggling doubt that freedom, in the personal sense, is a lost cause. It is revealing to compare Arthur Young's *The Mother-Lode* with Carl MacDougall's *Nocturne* and each in turn with the 'homeless' young narrator of Peter Chaloner's *Keen*.

At long last there are hopeful signs that several of the more original voices in prose fiction are beginning to call the tune of the times. Considerable talent lurks behind the heather-bells and the murky stumps of demolished tenements. There is a new willingness to experiment intelligently, and without indulgence, with familiar topics, subjects that must for a while remain the stuff of the Scottish dream and the genuine heritage of its writers.

Tradition has bequeathed us the tale; temperament the means of twisting it. If the stories selected for this volume are more than straws in the wind there is every reason for optimism regarding the state of the writer's craft in Scotland.

HUGH RAE

CHARLIE CHAPLIN'S SECRET

Graham Petrie

Charlie Chaplin comes out of his house, his hovel. He stands
on the doorstep and sniffs the gritty air of the city. His nose
wrinkles in disapproval. He eases his hands into his woollen
mitts. The holes in the mitts occupy more space than the
wool does and his fingers and hands remain essentially uncovered. He takes his cane from under his arm and adjusts
his bowler hat. Now he is ready to go. With a little skip and a
kick of his heels, he is off. He waddles down the street,
swinging his cane. Here are some of the things that he does on
his journey down the block. He steals an apple from an un-
tended fruit stall on the sidewalk and eats it. He chucks a baby
under the chin. He raises his hat in greeting to a pretty young
woman, who turns away from him with a shudder. He sniffs
the faded carnation in his button-hole. He pretends to kick a
policeman in the pants and cunningly avoids detection. He
finds a half-smoked cigar in the gutter, still smouldering, and
finishes it off with great enjoyment. He throws the butt away
just as he turns the corner and comes into the large square at
the centre of the city, where they are burning the woman.

The woman is aged about twenty-five and has blonde hair.
She is very pretty. When Chaplin looks at her, he is reminded
of the young lady to whom he tipped his hat a few moments
ago, but of course this is a different person entirely. He feels
that if he had smiled at this woman, she would have smiled
back rather than shrinking from him in disgust. She is poorly
dressed, in a faded white blouse and a torn skirt, and she
wears no shoes. She is probably as penniless as he is and, in

9

other circumstances, they might well have gone for a stroll in the park together, have sat together on a bench and shared a stolen apple. He begins to push his way through the crowd, to come closer to her, jostling the other spectators aside as he goes. When they protest at this treatment, he tips his hat to them in apology and continues on his way. Where necessary, he stamps on toes, kicks women in the shins, and digs his elbow into men's ribs. Finally he is at the front of the crowd, only a few feet away from the woman herself, but just at that moment someone thrusts a rag into her mouth to stop her from screaming and the Mayor leans forward and pokes a lighted torch into the bundle of sticks at her feet. Flames billow briefly upwards and then she is shrouded in smoke.

So there is nothing much to see after all and the disappointed crowd begins to disperse. Chaplin takes hold of one of his neighbours by the arm and detains him. 'What had she done?' he asks. The man shrugs. 'Who knows?' he replies. 'It could have been anything.' He pulls his arm free and joins the other spectators in their exodus. Chaplin gazes thoughtfully at the stake, where occasionally the smoke clears and he can glimpse a figure that has slumped forward, pressing against the ropes, her head resting on her breast. It seems to be over fairly quickly, he reflects. The smoke reaches them first and asphyxiates them before the flames catch hold upon their bodies. Horrible though it is, it is perhaps better than drowning. He remembers taking a stroll along the seashore just a week ago and noticing a crowd assembling at the water's edge. Once again they were watching a woman, this time tied to a stake fixed about twenty-five yards into the water. At this stage the water hardly reached her waist but, as the tide advanced it would, in perhaps an hour's time, cover her completely. This is a much slower process, he knows, though equally inexorable. He imagines the water reaching the chin, the struggle to raise the head higher, to gain a few extra minutes, the water lapping against the chin, the nostrils, retreating, advancing once more. He shakes his head. He had not stayed to watch, though many in the crowd had been there since dawn and would wait until nothing could be seen but the tip of the stake projecting above the waves.

He walks quickly away from the square, round the corner, and along the main street of the city. Past the magnificent circular fountain, with its three bronze horses rearing, its statue of Poseidon, and its water nymphs. A group of citizens are engaged in ducking a witch here, under the benign supervision of a policeman. The government provides, absolutely free of charge, a fruit stall for these occasions, at which small children can claim a supply of old eggs and rotten vegetables with which they pelt the witches in the intervals when they are allowed to recover their breath. This particular witch is near the end of her strength, and the men holding her shoulders have to haul her back out of the water after each submersion and slap her face to bring her back to consciousness for the next one. Chaplin does not stay long at this spectacle either; he steps back into the street and has to leap smartly aside almost immediately to avoid being mown down by a troop of soldiers who run past him at the double, holding their rifles ready for action. They are on their way to make an arrest and, a moment later, their officers follow, riding in a jeep, resplendent in their dark-green uniforms, their peaked, gold-braided caps.

Now he is hungry once again and it is time for him to find something to eat. He follows a mangy dog for some time, hoping that it might lead him to a hidden cache of food, but it takes him only to the pit where the bodies are thrown and lie uncovered all day, black with flies, until the bulldozers come to cover them up each evening. The dog is chased away from this by the guards and Chaplin turns away too, sickened by the stench that greets his nostrils. Back in the centre of the city, he finds a restaurant and, though he has no money, he goes in and sits down, trusting to his wits to turn the situation to his benefit. He orders a plate of soup and some bread and then, realizing that he has nothing further to lose, he adds the highest-priced dish on the menu. The waiter, a huge man with a bald head and the flattened nose of an ex-boxer, glares at him suspiciously and asks to see his money. Charlie raises his hand in mild and pained reproach. Surely the man trusts him? He waves his hand slightly to signal that he intends to give no further explanation. The waiter shrugs his shoulders and goes off to place the order. It is none of his business after all, and the manager can handle any problems. He returns a few moments later and serves the soup. Charlie raises the spoon delicately to his nostrils, sniffs the liquid. Moustache and eyebrows are raised in approbation. He nods. The waiter can go. The waiter has gone already and is receiving payment from the man at the next table. There is a hole in his right-hand trouser pocket and the coin falls through, bounces on the floor and rolls directly to Charlie's feet. Immediately he covers it with his shoe. Neither the waiter nor any of the customers have noticed. When the waiter moves off, Charlie stoops and pretends to tie up his shoelace, recovering the coin at the same time. The waiter returns, bringing the main course. His suspicions have revived and again he demands payment in advance. Charlie produces the coin with a flourish and hands it to him. The waiter examines it, tests it with his teeth, nods, places it in his pocket. It falls out again immediately and rolls to Charlie's feet. He puts his shoe on top of it. At this rate he could eat in the restaurant for a year.

The food is good. It is the first decent meal he has eaten in weeks and he intends to savour it. After a few mouthfuls, he leans back in his chair, sighs in contentment, and takes a slow look round the restaurant at the other customers. They are all much as he might expect to find in a place like this, except for a young woman sitting at a table near him. To be sure, she is dressed in rags, but her features are finer, her eyes more sensitive and intelligent, than those of any of the others. He realizes that she is gazing longingly at his plate and that her own meal seems to consist of a crust of bread and a glass of water. When she becomes aware that he has noticed her, she turns her head away hastily and starts to nibble her bread. Charlie snaps his fingers and summons the waiter. He points at the woman's table and tells him to bring her what he himself is eating. The waiter demands payment and Charlie hands over the coin once again. The waiter puts it in a different pocket this time and goes away. Charlie shrugs philosophically and continues with his meal.

The waiter brings the woman her food and puts it down in front of her. She stares at the plate in surprise and protests that she had never ordered this. The waiter jerks his thumb at Charlie's table and moves off. The woman gazes at Charlie in bewilderment and he opens his arms in an expansive gesture. 'Go ahead and eat,' he urges her. She looks at him a moment longer and then, famished, falls to. He watches her eat, with a look of pleasure on his face, and then, in leisurely fashion, finishes his own meal. He gets up from his chair, belches politely, wipes his mouth with his napkin, and moves over to the woman's table. He tips his hat and asks if he can join her. She urges him to sit down and, with his accustomed tact, he turns his head away as she gobbles the remainder of the food. The waiter stops to receive payment at the next table. He puts the coin in his right-hand pocket and it falls through the hole to land at Charlie's feet. He puts his shoe over it and gazes round suspiciously. No one has noticed, not even the woman. He chooses his time to pick up the coin and asks the woman, who has now finished eating, if she would like some coffee. She says she would and he summons the waiter and orders two coffees. The man demands payment and Charlie hands him the coin. The waiter puts it between his teeth, jerks at it, and it folds over like toffee. He hurls it angrily to the floor and stamps on it. He seizes Charlie by the collar of his shabby jacket, with both hands, and hustles him rapidly to the door. He kicks the door open and throws him out into the street. Charlie Chaplin rolls over and over on the concrete sidewalk of the city.

When he has finished rolling, he opens his eyes and sees that the woman is kneeling over him. She asks anxiously if he is hurt and he replies that of course he is, concrete is no feather bed, but he trusts that he will survive nonetheless. He eases himself to his feet and brushes the dirt and dust from his clothes. There are some tears and scratches now that were not evident before, but that is a small matter and of little consequence. He raises his hat, bows politely to the woman, and offers her his arm. With an ecstatic little kick of his heels and a flourish of his cane, he is ready to go, and they set off side by side.

He asks who she is and where she is from. She is unemployed, of course, the usual story all round. In from the country six months ago, a job here, a job there, domestic service, waitress, seamstress, delivering circulars, lower and lower in the spiral each time. Till, if he had not come along, she would certainly have thrown herself in the river. This is said without emotion, and is true. He pats her arm reassuringly. There is no need for that now, in fact there never is. A fatherly government has offered, in such circumstances, an easy and comfortable expiry in exchange for the gift of all healthy and undamaged organs. Surely she has heard of this? She shudders and makes no reply. To distract her, he draws attention to the guillotine that is nearing completion in another of the main squares of the city. It rises stark and bleak against the pink façade of the parliament buildings, which glow in the radiance of the mid-afternoon sunshine. The victim is present already, standing motionless between two armed guards; he surveys the proceedings with an air of total apathy. This time Chaplin knows the story and he tells it to the woman as they pause to contemplate the scene. The man was condemned for an insult to the Leader: he named his first-born child after him, and a year later, the boy was discovered to be mentally defective. The child will die too, of course, with the father. The scaffolding is finished now, and buckets and swabs are placed in the required areas by teenage girls in their colourful national costume. The guillotine is tested: there is a tremendous rattling and clanging as the blade rushes down, a thud as it bites into its wooden groove. A hiss of empty air as it glides past the blankness where the neck will be.

But they do not choose to watch this any longer, and have to push and urge their way through the crowd that has already gathered behind them. There is always something to do in the city, always something to watch, and, despite their poverty, the inhabitants never lack for entertainment and are rarely bored. He says that he will take her back to his hovel and she can spend the night there. Tomorrow they will try to find her some work. And where will *he* sleep? she asks. He shrugs. He is accustomed to the open air and loves to watch the twinkling stars. Besides, the dew refreshes him. They walk together through the empty streets. Everyone has gathered in the square and some time soon, in ten or twenty minutes, they will hear a massive roar of approval, a cry of jubilation that will fade into a universal sigh, scattering and dispersing over the city like swallows returning to their nests at night. Later, dusk will settle on the buildings, the lights will come on in the streets, the bulldozers will set to work to cover up the pits. Theatres, nightclubs and cinemas will open: balm to the wounds of day, they soothe the fretful citizens, iron out the wrinkles of unrest.

The hovel is set on a patch of deserted ground, a lonely tooth in the gaping mouth of the street. Redevelopment is due here and all has been levelled accordingly, save for this one building. In a day or two, a crane will snatch it without warning, raise it, crush it, splinter it to matchwood, and all will be clear for the apartments and offices to follow. So Chaplin believes, though in fact a cultural centre is due to rise in this spot, designed by and named after the Leader. Beethoven and Aeschylus will boom in this very spot where now, as he opens the door, a loose beam tumbles down to crack him smartly on the head. He jumps aside, takes off his hat, and rubs his skull ruefully. The woman, whose name, at this stage, hardly matters, comforts him. He begins to re-arrange the scanty furniture. A table with three legs, which wobbles ominously when dragged into the centre of the room. A chair which will collapse as soon as pressure is applied to it. A second chair, ditto. Some newspaper for a tablecloth. A knife and fork, which he wipes on his sleeve, to polish them. For the lady. He ushers her solicitously into her seat. And raises her apologetically from the floor a moment later. Same performance for the second chair. Well, they can always stand. And in any case, there is nothing to eat. He has been searching in the cupboard and there is not even a stale crust to be found. Suddenly there is a thunderous knocking at the door and, before he can answer it, it is kicked open by a military boot. Soldiers swarm all over the room, smashing what little furniture has remained intact. The officer asks to see the woman's identity card and nods as he examines it. Yes, this is the one, take her away. Charlie tries to intervene, but is hit in the face with a butt of a rifle and is knocked down. Blood flows from the corner of his mouth and down his chin. The woman is dragged out screaming. One of the soldiers consoles him. 'Don't worry, mate,' he tells him. 'She'll be back again tomorrow, good as new. Or even better.' He winks and goes out, slamming the door behind him. The loose beam, dislodged, tumbles down again and, meeting no resistance, continues to swing aimlessly, like a pendulum. The idyll is over.

Charlie Chaplin gets slowly to his feet. He wipes the blood from his chin and mechanically tries to straighten the broken furniture. He gives this up and goes over to the door, opens it, and stares outside. Dusk is settling on the city, the lights are coming on in the streets. He will have to hurry if he is not to be late for work. He sets off along the street, not so jaunty now, his cane trailing neglected on the sidewalk behind him. In front of him is a stall at which lottery tickets are being drawn. The crowd around it blocks the sidewalk and he is edged out on to the road, where, neglectful as ever, he is almost knocked over by a passing car. The blare of its horn fades as it hurtles on down the street. The lucky number is announced and the jubilant winner throws his arms in the air and waves his ticket, while his unsuccessful rivals turn away disconsolately. Never mind, their turn will come. He has won the privilege of carrying out the garrotting at noon to-morrow of an anarchist student: there were more applicants even than usual for this task. Chaplin continues on his way, but is blocked by a man selling the new series of tickets, for next week. He waves him aside. Certainly the job is well paid, and certainly he is penniless, but he has never much liked the way eyes pop and bulge as the throat constricts. 'I am nothing but a shadow,' he assures the man as he passes. 'Ignore me.'

Now he is walking through the main square of the city once more and, as he nears the centre, the clock on the bell-tower begins to strike seven. A door opens, a bronze figure four feet high emerges, he strikes the hour with a hammer on the shell of a bronze tortoise. Chaplin breaks into a run: he will have to hurry if he is to reach the cinema on time, and he has never run well or gracefully in his life. His large shoes impede him, causing him to trip and stumble. He has to push his way through the crowds strolling peacefully along, examining the lighted shop windows and their exotic contents, stopping to buy some cigarettes or coffee, sitting down for a drink in the elegant outdoor cafés. People gaze after him in astonishment or indignation; some send curses ringing after him, but he pays them no attention. He reaches the back entrance to the theatre at four minutes past seven, bangs the door open, and rushes along the narrow corridors until he is standing just behind the curtains, a diminutive figure peering upwards at the giants striding and romping above him. As he watches, he begins to grow, stretching in height and width and yet becoming curiously flatter and less substantial, a being with no depth. This process is completed at just the moment when he is due to make his entrance: he marches boldly out into the screen, assimilating himself to its surface. He tips his hat to the heroine, a frail blonde woman, dressed in rags, and proceeds to chastise the policeman who is harassing her, kicking him impudently in the pants. The audience erupt into laughter. This is Charlie at last, they assure each other, poking and nudging with their elbows. Who for a few brief moments will avenge them. Charlie Chaplin, on whom the moon shines bright.

FATHER AND SON

Bernard MacLaverty

Because I do not sleep well, I hear my father rising to go to work. I know that in a few minutes he will come in to look at me sleeping. He will want to check that I am in. He will stand in his bare feet, his shoes and socks in his hand, looking at me. I will sleep for him. I will hear the snap of the switch on the kettle downstairs. I will hear him not eating anything and going about the kitchen with a stomach full of wind. He will come again to look at me before he goes out to his work. He will want a conversation. He stands breathing through his nose, with an empty lunch-box in the crook of his arm, looking at me.

Here lies my son who let me down. I love him so much it hurts, but he won't talk to me. He tells me nothing.

Wake up, son. I'm away to my work.

I hear you groan and see your eyes flicker open.

What are you going to do today?

What's it to you?

If I know what you're doing I don't worry about it.

O.K. I'll read a book.

A dirty one?

Shit.

My son, he turns away from me, a heave of bedclothes in his wake.

I do not sleep. My father does not sleep. The sound of ambulances criss-crosses the hours of dark. I sleep with the daylight. It is safe. At night I hear his bare feet click as he lifts them, walking the lino. The front door shudders as he leaves.

19

My son is breaking my heart. It is already broken. Is it my fault there is no woman in the house? Is it my fault a good woman should die? His face was never softer than when after I had shaved. A baby pressed to my shaved cheek. Now his chin is sandpaper. He is a man. When he was a boy I took him fishing. I taught him how to tie a blood knot, how to cast a fly, how to strike so the fish would not escape. How to play a fish. The green bus to quiet days in Toome. Him, pestering me with questions.

If I leave him alone he will break my heart anyway. I must speak to him. Tonight at tea. If he is in.

Early tonight?
You should be in bed. A man of your age. It's past one.
There's tea in the pot.
The boy shrugs and sits down. He takes up a paper between him and his father.
What do you be doing out to this time?
Not again.
Answer me.
Talking.
Who with?
Friends.
Do you want me to pour you your tea?
Naw, just go on to bed, Da, will you?
What do you talk about?
Nothing much.
Talk to me, son.
What about?
My son he looks confused. I want you to talk to me the way I hear you talk to people at the door. I want to hear you laugh with me like you used to. I want to know what you think. I want to know if you are in any danger. I want to know why you do not eat more. No more than pickings for four weeks. Your face is thin. Your fingers orange with nicotine. I

pulled you away from death once and now you will not talk
to me.

About . . .

You haven't shaved yet.

I'm just going to. The water for the tea is still hot
enough.

Why do you shave at night?

Because in the morning my hand shakes.

Your hand shakes in the morning, because you're a coward.
You think the world is waiting round the corner to blow your
head off. A breakfast of two valium and the rest of them
rattling in your pocket, walking down the street to your work.
Won't answer the door without looking out the bedroom
window first. He's scared of his own shadow.

Son, you are living on borrowed time. Your hand shook
when you got home. I have given you the life you now have. I
fed you soup from a spoon when your own hand would have
spilled it. Let me put my arm around your shoulders and let
me listen to what is making you thin. At the week-end I will
talk to him.

It is hard to tell if his bed has been slept in. It is always
rumpled. I have not seen my son for two days. Then, on the
radio, I hear he is dead. They give out his description. I drink
milk. I cry.

But he comes in for his tea.

Why don't you tell me where you are?

Because I never know where I am.

My mother is dead but now I have another one in her place.
He is an old woman. He has been crying. I know he prays for
me all the time. He used to dig the garden, grow vegetables
and flowers for half the street. He used to fish. To take me
fishing. Now he just waits. He sits and waits for me and the
weeds have taken over. I would like to slap his face and make
a man of him.

I let you go once – and look what happened.

Not this again.

The boy curls his lip as if snagged on a fish hook.

For two years I never heard a scrape from you. I read of London in the papers. Watched scenes from London on the News, looking over the man's shoulder at people walking past. I know you, son, you are easily led. Then a doctor phoned for me at work. The poshest man I ever spoke to.

I had to go and collect you. Like a dog.

The boy has taken a paper up. He turns the pages noisily, crackling like fire.

A new rig-out from Littlewoods.

Socks, drawers, shirt, the lot. In a carrier bag. The doctor said he had to burn what was on you. I made you have your girl's hair cut. It was Belfast before we spoke. You had the taint of England in your voice.

Today I thought you were dead.

Every day you think I am dead. You live in fear. Of your own death. Peeping behind curtains, the radio always loud enough to drown any noise that might frighten you, double-locking doors. When you think I am not looking you hold your stomach. You undress in the dark for fear of your shadow falling on the window blind. At night you lie with the pillow over your head. By your bed, a hatchet which you pretend to have forgotten to tidy away. I know a mouse with more courage.

Well I'm not.

Why don't you tell me where you go?

Look Da. I have not touched the stuff since I came back. Right?

Why don't you have a girl like everybody else?

Oh fuck.

He bundles the paper and hurls it in the corner and stamps up the stairs to his room. The old man shouts at the closed door.

Go and wash your mouth out.

He cries again staring at the ceiling so that the tears run down to his ears.

My son, he is full of hatred. For me, for everything. He spits when he speaks, when he shouts his voice breaks high and he is like a woman, he grinds his teeth and his skin goes white about his mouth. His hands shake. All because I ask him where he goes. Perhaps I need to show him more love. Care for him more than I do.

I mount the stairs quietly to apologize. My son, I am sorry. I do it because I love you. Let me put my arm around you and talk like we used to on the bus from Toome.

The door swings open and he pushes a handgun beneath the pillow. Seen long enough, black and squat, dull like a garden slug. He sits, my son, his hands idling, empty, staring hatred.

Why do you always spy on me, you nosey old bastard. His voice breaks, his eyes bulge.

What's that? Under the pillow?

It's none of your fucking business.

He kicks the door closed in my face with his bare foot. I am in the dark of the landing. I must pray for him. On my bended knees I will pray for him to be safe. Perhaps I did not see what I saw. Maybe I was mistaken. My son rides pillion on a motor-bike. Tonight I will not sleep. I do not think I will sleep again.

It is ten o'clock. The News begins. The old man stands drying a plate, watching the headlines. There is a ring at the door. The son answers it, his shirt-tail out. Voices in the hallway.

My son with friends. Talking. What he does not do with me.

There is a bang. The old man drops the dishcloth and runs to the kitchen door. He puts his head around the door and looks into the hallway. His son is lying on the floor, his head on the bottom stair, his feet on the threshold. There is no one else. The News has come to my door. The old man runs to his son.

Are you hurt?

Blood is spilling from his nose.

They have punched you and you are not badly hurt. Your nose is bleeding. Something cold at the back of your neck.

He takes his son's head in his hands and sees a hole in his nose that should not be there. At the base of his nostril and he knows that the hole goes up into his brains.

My son, let me put my arms around you.

MOTHER AND DAUGHTER

James Shaw Grant

I had never been at an island funeral before. I knew the
island well, however, and it did not surprise me that the
whole village stopped work for the day. There was no one
turning hay on the crofts, or taking home peats, and no wash-
ing on the line anywhere, although dry days are precious in
high summer in the west.

Indeed, there was some criticism of my friend, Kenneth,
because he went to work as usual in the school at Craignure
where he teaches Mathematics. Craignure is twenty miles
away, but he is still regarded as a member of the community
in Fiskavaig where he lives with his mother. Had he been a
doctor, it would have been different: education falls in the
category of things the islander regards as supremely valuable
but not essential, and so not free from the prohibition in the
Fourth Commandment on Sabbath work, or from those
social customs of the village which, through long years of use
and wont, have come to acquire the same implicit sanctity,
although they do not rest on Holy Writ as interpreted by the
Westminster Confession of Faith.

It did surprise me that there were no women in the
funeral procession. They were present at the service in the
house, but they watched discreetly from the windows as the
men took the bier in orderly rotation, as if directed by some
invisible and inaudible sergeant-major, and carried it across a
mile of broken moor from Bellag's miserable cottage to the
public road.

When the road was reached, the coffin was placed on the
floor of an ancient bus from which the seats had been tem-

porarily removed, and the procession continued on wheels to the cemetery at Skigersta where Bellag was laid to rest in the golden sand, surrounded by one of the finest panoramas of sea and mountain in Europe, to which, as I judged by my limited acquaintanceship with her, she was no more insensitive in death than she had been in life.

A resting place fit for a king, and a public funeral in which the whole community took part, for an ancient recluse whom the very old regarded with some apprehension as a witch, and the young as an eccentric they were free to torment with catcalls and practical jokes, or perhaps felt impelled to torment by some primitive defence mechanism against the maverick who stood apart from the rest of the tribe. Most of the villagers had no strong feelings about Bellag, they accepted her as she was, but, as she avoided them, they paid little attention to her until she died, when they rallied round to ensure that she had a decent burial, according to the custom of the island, down even to the service of whisky and biscuits which materialized from nowhere at the graveside to refresh the mourners after the labour of carrying the coffin and digging the grave, for there was no gravedigger or custodian, and the cemetery was almost unvisited by man, except when a burial was taking place – which I always thought surprising in an island so much more preoccupied with death and ancestry on one hand and a remote eternity on the other, than with the here and now, although in the here and now, giving the paradox another twist, they were immensely practical.

What a fitting end to an uneventful life, I thought, as I sipped my whisky by the cemetery gate, and enjoyed the palpable peace of the Hebrides, where sound and silence are not incompatible and mutually destructive, as they are in the busy haunts of men, but two separate qualities of the environment which coexist in harmony, enhancing each other, so that the quiet is heightened by the song of the unseen lark, or the dull roar of the Atlantic on the beach behind the dunes.

'I always thought she was like the stones of which her thatched cottage was built,' I said to Kenneth in the evening, elaborating my theme. 'Old and grey and unchanging, touched by nothing except wind and rain, weathering imperceptibly. And self-contained. Touching the neighbouring stones in the wall but unaffected by them, although I suppose even a stone is changed in some way by the pressure of the stones around it.'

'If it comes to that,' said Kenneth, 'the stones were formed in a cataclysm such as we have not known in our lifetime and which, if it occurred again, we certainly could not survive.'

'Meaning?' I enquired.

'There are two errors implicit in what you have been saying,' replied Kenneth, very deliberately, as if picking his way across a bit of boggy ground. 'You assume that life in a village like Fiskavaig is devoid of incident because everything seems so placid on the surface. You also assume that you know all about Bellag just because you have visited her, eaten her scones, drunk her tea, and listened to her stories, in an effort, I may say, to demonstrate that you are above the petty prejudices of the natives.'

'That's unfair,' I snapped. 'I visited Bellag because I found her more interesting than anyone else in the village. She may have been a recluse but she had a treasury of old songs and stories that was absolutely priceless. Her neighbours, who might have shared it because they shared the same background and tradition, threw it away, and despised her for trying to preserve it. With Bellag's death, Fiskavaig has lost the one thing that raised it above the commonplace.'

'That may be true,' said Kenneth. 'But I am not talking of tradition. I am talking of fact. Or rather the absence of fact. Not even those of us who have lived here all our lives know

Bellag's story. Not even those who were here when it happened are sure beyond a peradventure.'

'When what happened?' I asked him.

'That's just the point,' he said. 'When what happened?'

He paused for a moment. Then he asked me, 'Did you notice anything peculiar about the family mourners at the funeral?'

I had, and I had intended to ask him about it. They were obviously twins, but I could not think what their relationship to Bellag might be. I knew she had a son who was drowned along with his father when fishing lobsters, leaving Bellag in a state of penury which would have been beyond anything that could exist today were it not for the kindness of her neighbours, which she always acknowledged, although she obviously hated them for other things. She told me once how she worried when her menfolk failed to return for their evening meal and at last got out the telescope which her husband had from the days when he had been a gamekeeper.

'I looked up the loch and I looked down the loch,' she had said to me, 'and I saw nothing. Then I looked again and, in the gloaming, I saw a boat, and its keel was pointing to the sky, and there was a cap on the water beside it. And then I knew there was no man left of all my relations to turn the croft for me while I was alive or take me to the graveyard when I died.'

When I suggested gently that she could hardly have identified a cap at such a distance even with a telescope, she replied, 'It was just a little black speck rising on the wave and going down again. I could not see it was a cap, but I knew it was a cap, and the villagers brought it back to me, and it is still hanging in the closet today, and that is all that is left to me of my husband or my son, for to tell you the truth I don't know which of them was wearing it when they went out that morning, because they had only one between the two of them.'

All this passed quickly through my mind before I replied to Kenneth's query about the mourners. 'They are obviously twins,' I said, 'and they obviously hate each other's guts, but how are they related to Bellag?'

Kenneth took some time to reply. 'Whatever else they are, they're not twins,' he said. 'All we know in Fiskavaig is that they were born within a few weeks of each other, one of them to Bellag and the other to her daughter Mary.'

'She never told me she had a daughter,' I exclaimed.

'Mary disappeared not long after the children were born. It was a mean thing to do, leaving the old woman to cope with her daughter's child as well as her own. So far as I know, Bellag never mentioned her daughter's name after that to anyone. She seems to have blotted her completely from memory.'

Not completely, I thought to myself, because an odd idea had struck me, but I was still not sure enough to mention it to Kenneth. 'Who fathered them?' I asked him.

'Very cleverly put,' he replied. 'You've dodged the use of either singular or plural. And that's what we don't know for sure. They both take their dominant features from their mothers, but they could hardly be so alike if they did not have the same father. Unless, of course, there was a very close relationship between the fathers just as there was between the mothers.'

'That's just too ridiculous,' I suggested. 'In a small place like Fiskavaig people are bound to know.'

'Lots of us believe we know,' said Kenneth. 'But there are several different schools of thought on the subject, each with its own answer. It's odd how people tend to become more positive in their assertions the less proof they have.'

I suggested that we should leave the question of paternity aside for a moment, and gave him just the slightest hint that I might be in possession of some relevant facts which he did not have, even although up to that moment I had not been aware of the situation to which my facts related. He was very surprised, but he did not press me to a premature disclosure of what I knew or suspected, and he patiently answered my questions about the two mysterious mourners.

After Mary disappeared, he told me, Bellag brought the two boys up like brothers. They had, to all appearances, a happy childhood, despite their poverty. You could see them together on the hill, laughing and playing as they herded the village cattle. They were the liveliest boys of their age when there was a gathering or a dipping or some idle ploy afoot.

They were always ready to go together to help a neighbour with the peats. None of the other lads were so successful when it came to birds'-nesting: they were absolutely fearless on the cliffs. And when one of the boats wanted a young lad as an extra hand for a night's fishing, they were the first choice, but it was always a problem because one would not go without the other and, even if there were berths available on two of the boats on the same day, it was difficult to prise them apart.

Then, quite suddenly, it all changed. It was Sunday, and the boys were at church together. There was an air of expectancy over the congregation because two young lovers were to be publicly reproved. They were shortly to be married, but first they had to undergo humiliation on the stool of repentance.

The minister, John MacCullich, was notorious for his savagery on these occasions. He was a huge man, with arms like a gorilla: domineering, ruthless, coarse-mouthed, but with a lively sense of humour which set the congregation tittering even when they burned with indignation at his verbal assault on them all in the mass, or were moved by pity for some specific victim of his brutal wit. He was never more eloquent, funnier or coarser than when he was chastising a young couple for what he termed pre-marital fornication, and these sermons had a special piquancy, because his own reputation with women was far from savoury, although nothing was ever proved against him. Every word of his sermon was relished for several shades of meaning at once, and the congregation generally left the church chuckling at the wisecracks, gloating self-righteously over the victims while envying them their recklessness and pitying them for the punishment at the same time, and admiring the preacher for his undoubted panache even while they hated him as a bully and despised him as a hypocrite.

On this occasion, he excelled himself and the congregation sat enthralled. They were enjoying simultaneously the sadistic pleasure of the mob at the Roman circus when the lions were loosed on the helpless captives, and the fun of a rollicking French farce crammed with compromising situations, broad innuendoes and downright bawdry until, carried away by his eloquence, MacCullich said things for which the congregation never forgave him, even though the sermon passed into local folklore and was many times recalled in after years round a peat fire like some old battle of the Fenians.

It was no wonder, he thundered, that the young men and women of the village lived unashamedly in sin when they had before them for many years the example of a woman taken in adultery in her widow's weeds, who had brought her daughter up so loosely that she was taken in adultery too.

The offence, he said, was flagrant, and it was compounded by the fact that neither mother nor daughter had ever come to the stool of repentance. The daughter had vanished from their midst, no doubt to pursue her life of self-indulgence in the cities of the plain, while the mother remained sullenly aloof from her neighbours and never darkened the doorstep of the church.

Then he turned squarely on the two young lads who were regular attenders at church in spite of Bellag's abstinence. Pointing his finger directly at them, he prophesied that the wrath of God would follow them throughout life because the sins of the parents were visited on the children and they were twice accursed. The fact that Bellag had lost her husband and her son in a drowning on the same day, he declared, was a judgement falling on her even before the commission of the crime because crime and punishment alike had been fore-ordained from the beginning of the world.

The congregation was aghast. Up until then, there had been a tacit understanding in the village that, however much speculation there might be about the paternity of the lads, nothing should be said in their presence to set them asking questions or break the unusual relationship which bound them so closely together.

Although MacCullich pointed directly at them, the lads did not seem at first to take the tirade to themselves but, when they did, they rose together silently and walked from the church. They had arrived together and sat together, as they always did, but they left through different doors, and after that no one in the village ever again saw the two of them together. If one came into the ceilidh house and found the other there, he turned and went away again, unless the other had seen him first and slipped out quietly through the peat smoke before the newcomer's eyes had adjusted to the haze. They stopped taking their meals together: they either went to different ends of the house with their porridge, or potatoes and herring, or one of them lingered outside until the other had done. Up till then they had shared the same bed but, from that night on, neither of them went near it. God knows where they slept, but it was obvious from their appearance that they roughed it. They had to sit in the same room at school, but they never spoke to each other in the class or in the playground and, although they had both been really bright and anxious to get on, hardly a day passed without one of them playing truant, though oddly they were never both missing on the same day. It was almost as if they were both still anxious to get all the schooling they could so long as they did not have to meet. They must have kept a very close watch on each other because they never by accident both asked to go out on the same boat, and they never turned up at the same fank or the same wedding, although on every village occasion one of them was there.

The villagers, said Kenneth, never really knew which of the lads was present at any given time. They were both called Donald, although they were never christened, and naturally they both used the same surname. The only distinguishing mark was a slight difference in height, a fraction of an inch, just enough to permit the villagers, a little derisively, to call them Big Donald and Little Donald, although you could only be certain which was which when you saw the two of them together, and even then, only Bellag knew which was whose son.

When they finally left home, they went on the same day – or almost. They seem to have made up their minds at the same time, and they both walked into Drumbeg to get the steamer for the mainland but, when one saw the other already on the gangway, he turned on his heel and walked the twenty miles back home again, to wait for the next steamer two days later.

Neither of them came back to Fiskavaig, even for a short holiday. Occasionally, very occasionally, word filtered through that one of them had been seen by a seaman, or someone who had emigrated from Fiskavaig or one of the villages round about, but these chance meetings were rare: unlike most islanders away from home, they seemed to avoid rather than seek out other islanders living in the same vicinity.

'I would say from their hats and their accents,' said Kenneth, 'that both of them settled in America. It is certainly in America they were last seen by anyone from Fiskavaig.'

As far as I noticed, they did not speak to each other at the graveside, and said little to the villagers who crowded round to condole with them and shake them by the hand. They were not discourteous to the villagers, but they obviously did not want to be drawn into conversation or to answer the questions that were showered upon them.

'What I can't understand,' said Kenneth, 'is how, if they live in America, they knew the old lady had died. They must have heard at once or they could not possibly have been here in time for the funeral.'

'That part of the problem is simply solved,' I told him. 'I sent them a cable. Not directly. Indeed, I did not know they existed, but Bellag asked me, many months ago, when she first realized she was really ill, to send a cable at once, if anything happened to her, to two addresses she gave me scribbled on a piece of paper. One address was in New York. The other in Houston.'

I took the scrap of paper from my pocket and passed it to him, but it did not reveal very much. In each case, the address was that of a legal firm.

'It's odd,' I said to Kenneth, 'that when she was so meticulous about informing both the sons, she did not send a message to her daughter too. She must have lost all trace of Mary.'

'Mary just vanished,' said Kenneth. 'There was a lot of talk about it at the time. It was assumed she left by the mail steamer but no one actually saw her on board and, although the boys have been seen once or twice over the years, as I have told you, I have never heard of anyone who came across Mary.'

'Are you sure she did leave Fiskavaig?' I asked him. I put the question reluctantly because I was afraid my imagination was running away with me, but I had an irresistible urge to go on probing.

'What makes you ask that?' he said sharply, as if he sensed there was more behind my question than idle curiosity.

'Perhaps I should not say this,' I replied. 'It is all too fanci-

34

ful, but I must get it out of my system, and perhaps what I really need is a little cold water from a cool calculating mathematician like yourself.'

'Go on,' he coaxed, as I hesitated, gazing into the heart of the peat fire, trying to sharpen my memory and order my thoughts.

Over the years I had known her, I had noted down from Bellag many ancient tales which she told me in English, although she obviously knew them and remembered them only in Gaelic. Though I am a fair linguist, it was more than I could do, to recall a story in my mother tongue and tell it in a foreign language with almost equal fluency, apart from the occasional idiom transliterated from one language to the other which, together with the simplicity and stiffness of her English vocabulary, gave Bellag's stories a pleasantly archaic flavour which heightened the effect.

There was one story to which I had paid no special attention at the time, but it came back into my mind as I spoke with Kenneth, vaguely at first, but then more insistently, as I recalled the details. It was the story of a legendary Norwegian queen and her only daughter. It had all the characteristic trappings of the traditional tale: the repetitions, the stereotyped but vivid descriptions of the dramatis personae, the language, not poetic, but heightened above the language of ordinary conversation and obviously designed to be easily remembered. For instance, she described the Queen as having the beauty of the sun on a winter's evening, riding majestically over the western ocean 'as if she were clothed in rubies and in fire', in contrast with the daughter whose beauty was like the moon on a frosty night 'walking gracefully among the stars in a gauze of light'. And then there was the mysterious lover who came to them across the mountains and wore the simple habit of a hermit or a priest, but underneath it 'the silver breastplate of a man of power and ruthlessness and might', and they did not know whether he came from some distant part of the country or from Elfland or from the deepest pit, but every word he spoke was so sweet it took their sense away and he wooed them both, each without the knowledge of the other.

I could sense Kenneth's interest as I tried to rebuild the story from memory. I did not have my notebooks with me, and the manner in which I recalled the tale was obviously influenced by the parallel between it and Bellag's own circumstances. I just hoped, as I spoke, that my memory was not playing tricks on me and that I was not shaping the story to suit the point I wished to make as so many of us quite unconsciously do.

According to Bellag's telling of the story, the Queen had lost her husband in a Viking raid, and the stranger came to her first with tidings of his death and words of consolation. Although she did not know him, she received him as a friend of her husband and she loved him first for the love he seemed to have had for him. Her daughter loved him more directly for his handsome face and gallant bearing.

Even if she had not loved him, the Queen would have wished to marry him; she needed a strong man to help her rule her kingdom and, although she knew her nobles would resent her marrying so soon and marrying a stranger, it seemed to her easier than choosing one of themselves and arousing the enmity of all the rest. She met him in secret and accepted his love for fear of losing him, but she put off any plans for marriage or public disclosure of her love until she realized that concealment was no longer possible.

On the day that she decided to summon her nobles and announce her marriage, she realized for the first time that she had a rival for the stranger's affection and that her daughter was in the same sad plight as herself.

Strangely (as Bellag told the tale) there was no enmity at first between them. They wept on each other's shoulders, and sought consolation together. They helped each other to face the nobles and resist the censure of the Church. To the love of mother and daughter was added a different kind of love as if they were sisters as well, sisters in affliction.

And then one day, after the children were born, they quarrelled. Although they had been betrayed and deserted, each still secretly loved her betrayer, and each still hoped he would return one day to marry her. The Queen needed a husband more than ever now to control the nobles, and the daughter still longed with passion for the lover who had brought her so much secret joy.

The Queen had told her daughter that she must marry for reasons of state and any affection the daughter had for the mysterious knight must be set aside; the daughter acquiesced, or at least appeared to, but in the darkness she tried to slip secretly from the palace and seek her lover across the mountains, although she had no idea where to find him. The Queen saw her and had her intercepted. After that, the bitterness between them was greater even than the love had been, and the mother jealously watched the daughter night after night.

Some months passed in this cat and mouse enmity, according to Bellag's tale, before the daughter found another opportunity. This time, she got clean away, but her mother followed her into the mountains by her footprints in the snow. She did not overtake her but the footprints ended abruptly on the edge of a fearsome precipice. There was no doubt, said Bellag, from the marks in the snow, which could be seen quite clearly in the moonlight, that the daughter had lost her foothold and was lying at the bottom of the cliff hundreds of feet below, where not even the birds could peck her bleaching bones.

Bellag presumably did not know the word crevasse, nor did she use the English 'crevice', although that was what I visualized as she told the tale: she spoke rather of 'a great hole in the side of the mountain like a pot, so deep you could not see the bottom but could hear the water boiling far below'.

This flashed irrelevantly into my mind as I gave Kenneth a shortened version of Bellag's tale, but I did not pause to elaborate. I wanted to hurry on to the point which seemed to me of more direct significance, and I used Bellag's precise words which remained clearly in my memory.

'The Queen, who had loved her daughter as no mother had ever loved a daughter before, returned home rejoicing because her rival was dead, but though she sent couriers secretly into all the countries round about, they never discovered who the Queen's lover had been, and he never came back to redeem his promise.'

Bellag then went on to describe in great detail the upbringing and friendship of the two boys, and although it was a story of horses and hawks and hunting in the forest, and feasting with nobles in the palace at night, the parallel was unmistakable with Kenneth's prosaic account of the youth in Fiskavaig of Bellag's own son and grandson.

I could not, without reference to my notes, recall how in Bellag's tale the boys had discovered their strange relationship but, just as had happened in real life, they quarrelled and parted.

'Their quarrel broke the old Queen's heart, but the one rode north and the other rode south, and while she lived they never again turned their horses' heads towards each other or the place from whence they had fled, but each became a great prince in the land to which he went, and both of them paid tribute to the Queen, whom each regarded as his own mother.

'When the Queen died, she was by far the richest of the rulers in that part of the country, and the nobles quarrelled and fought over the gold in her treasure house, which was more than they imagined existed in the whole of the world. But, as they fought, a horseman came riding out of the north and a horseman came riding out of the south, and they had armed men at their backs, and the nobles were driven from the treasure house without a dust of gold to show for their greed.

'The nobles gathered outside the treasure house and made peace with each other and formed a band to drive the strangers out and get the gold again. But though they called them strangers they knew they were the brothers come back to claim their own, but they had always hated them just as they hated the Queen for her love of the knight with the silver breastplate.

'While they were still planning the attack, a great flame spread across the sky and they realized the treasure house was ablaze. Never in that country was seen so fierce a fire and, in the morning, when it had spent itself, there was nothing to be seen among the ruins but two charred skeletons, each with a dagger stuck in its breast. And there was not a trace to be found of the jewels or the gold.

' "They killed each other," said one of the nobles, who was not renowned for his wisdom, but the Queen's chief counsellor replied, "That is as it may be, but whoever heard of a fire that could destroy not only the crown and the chalice, but the very gold itself and the gems with which it was adorned?" And they fled from the place because then they knew, for the first time, that the Queen's lover had been the Wicked One himself.'

By the time I finished, I felt quite exhausted with the effort of trying to recall Bellag's tale and, as far as possible, her precise language.

'The Wicked One,' said Kenneth reflectively, and then, after a pause, he added, 'I haven't been in Bellag's house for years.'

'But you want to go across with me in the morning,' I suggested.

'Yes,' said Kenneth, with a hesitant smile, 'just to make sure that it hasn't vanished overnight in a flash of lightning.'

'There's not much fear of that,' I said; 'although Bellag seems to have woven a mock traditional tale out of the events of her life, she could not be expected to foresee what would happen at her own death, and there certainly wasn't much sign of riches in the home she lived in, nor the way she lived there.'

'That's true,' said Kenneth. 'But a horseman did come out of the north, so to speak, and another out of the south' – and, although we were both sceptics where the supernatural is concerned, we were just a little disappointed, and perhaps even a little surprised, in the morning to find that Bellag's house was where we left it: no sign there of a fierce destroying fire.

But, when we opened the door, the house was in confusion. Every corner had been frantically ransacked. Bellag's few sticks of furniture were tumbled and smashed, as if there had been a furious fight. Lying with his head in the ashes of the burnt-out peat fire was one of the brothers with a bread knife stuck between his ribs. The other was behind the door with a bullet in his back. We had difficulty opening the door because of the body slumped against it.

In a corner of the room, as if it had slithered there when the table was smashed in the mêlée, was an old tin biscuit box, with the framed pictures of George V and Queen Mary still showing vaguely through the rust, and in the box were ten thousand dollars in high denomination notes.

We should have left everything untouched before we sent for the police, but what had happened was all too clear, and we had other important questions on our minds that the law was not concerned with.

The notes in the biscuit box were still neatly stowed in the packages in which they had come. Some of the packages bore a New York postmark and the others were from Houston, Texas. The writing on the envelopes was so similar you could have sworn they were written by the same hand, and the tally of each group was the same, as if the love the young men had borne her was precisely equal even when measured in dollar bills.

But it was not the money they had fought over. There had also been, presumably in the same tin box, an envelope with two birth certificates. Half of the envelope was clutched in the cold hand of the corpse by the fire and the other half by the corpse at the door, as if they had pulled a Christmas cracker, hoping that out of it would come, not a paper hat and a corny wisecrack, but the truth about their own identity. It was a forlorn hope because, when we put the pieces together, there was still no way of knowing to which of the dead men each certificate related.

A few days later, when the police were done with their purposeless enquiries, there was another funeral in Fiskavaig, a double funeral in which there were no family mourners but, before the coffins were closed, the two corpses were carefully measured by some of the neighbours, and the coffins marked, so that, later, they were able to erect a little stone on each of the graves with no inscription but the names 'Donald Mor' and 'Donald Beag'.

They prepared the graves in opposite corners of the cemetery, well away from Bellag's own, because no one could say which was the son and which the grandson, so that they did not know how to place them in the family plot.

In accord with the local practice, there was no service by the graveside and no prayers for the dead, but MacCullich, now an old man, white-haired and beginning to stoop, conducted a service at the house. Having known him only through Kenneth's account of the brothers' quarrel, I was surprised at the quiet and reverent manner in which he prayed, and prayed with obvious sincerity, for all those assembled at the funeral who were themselves burdened with guilt, and wished to be reconciled with their neighbours and their God before death overtook them unexpectedly as it had the two they were burying that day, who had died in anger, each by the other's hand.

It was when I looked out my notes of Bellag's tale after the funerals and went through them with Kenneth, that he interrupted me excitedly, 'We have another investigation to make. By God, I wonder!'

He told me then that Bellag's description of what I took to be a crevasse fitted exactly the notorious seal hole by the path along the cliff top from Fiskavaig to Marvig. There was no one now living in Marvig because it was remote from the main road, but, in his youth, there had been two or three fisher families there. In fact, he said, it was the Marvig folk who had recovered the bodies of Bellag's husband and her son.

'They were great seamen, but uncouth,' he said. 'When they gave up the sea, several of them went into the professions and did well, though they never acquired the graces. MacCullich was one, and he's still more at home in a boat in a gale than preaching in a pulpit or praying by a sickbed.'

The seal hole is unfenced. A great gaping hole in the moor, a hundred feet deep or more. You cannot see the bottom but, as it is connected with the sea by an underground passage, you can hear the eerie swish of breaking waves beneath your feet. There is no memory in Fiskavaig of any accident at the seal hole, but when Kenneth and I got ropes and descended, we found on a ledge at the bottom the unmistakable skeleton of a young woman.

'So that's how Mary disappeared,' said Kenneth, and we both had a vivid picture in our minds of the daughter fleeing along the cliff path in the snow, pursued by her jealous mother.

It was only then I handed to Kenneth the photograph I had taken from the bottom of the biscuit box, where it had been hidden beneath the bundles of notes. It was of a handsome young man in a fisherman's jersey, and written on the back was the message, 'Meet me on Friday if you can sneak out when the old bitch is asleep.'

Was that the cause of the quarrel, or did Bellag only find it after Mary was dead? Was it written before the children were born, or afterwards? Was it the invitation which led the daughter to her death?

We will never know, but of one thing Kenneth and I had no doubt – we recognized the photograph.

CHRISTIAN ENDEAVOUR

Alan Spence

I had been a religious fanatic for only a few weeks.

'What is it the night then?' asked my father. 'The bandy hope?' I caught the mockery, but he meant no harm.

'Christian Endeavour,' I said, drying my face with a towel and stretching up to peer at myself in the cracked mirror above the sink. 'Band a Hope's on Thursday.'

The two halves of my face in the mirror didn't quite match because of the crack, were slightly out of alignment. It was an old shaving-mirror of my father's with an aluminium rim, hung squint from a nail in the window-frame.

'Ah thought Christian Endeavour was last night?'

'That was just the Juniors,' I said. 'Tonight's the Real one.'

'Are ye no too young?' said my father.

'The minister says ah can come.'

'Is that because ye were top in the bible exam?'

'Top equal,' I said. 'Ah don't know if that's why. He just said ah could come.'

'Ach well,' said my father, going back behind his news-paper. 'Keeps ye aff the streets.'

'Ah'll be the youngest there,' I said, proud of myself and wanting to share it.

'Mind yer heid in the door,' he said. 'It's that big ye'll get stuck.'

I pulled on my jacket and was ready to go.

'Seen ma bible?' I asked.

'Try lookin where ye left it,' he said.

I found it on the table with another book, *The Life of David*

Livingstone, under the past week's heap of newspapers and comics. The book had been my prize in the bible exam.

The exam had been easy. Questions like *Who carried Christ's cross on the way to Calvary?* And from the Shorter Catechism, *Into what estate did the fall bring mankind?*

It was just a matter of remembering.

The label gummed in the book read FIRST PRIZE, with EQUAL penned in above BIBLE KNOWLEDGE, and then my name.

My father remembered reading the same book as a boy. He had been a sergeant in the Boys' Brigade, and the book had made him want to be a missionary himself.

'Great White Doctor an that,' he said. 'Off tae darkest Africa.'

But somehow he had drifted away from it all. 'Wound up in darkest Govan instead,' he said.

For the years he had been in the Boys' Brigade, he had been given a long-service badge. I still kept it in a drawer with a hoard of other badges I had gathered over the years. Most of them were cheap tin things, button badges: ABC Minors, Keep Britain Tidy. But the BB badge was special, heavier metal in the shape of an anchor. I had polished it with Brasso till it shone. There were two other treasures in the drawer: an army badge an uncle had given me, shaped like a flame, and a Rangers supporters badge, a silver shield with the lion rampant in red.

Christian Endeavour had a badge of its own. A dark blue circle with a gold rim, and CE in gold letters. The Sunday-school teachers at the Mission all wore it. I had been disappointed that there wasn't one for the Juniors. But now that I was moving up, I would be entitled to wear the badge. CE. In gold.

'Is ther gonnae be any other youngsters there the night?' asked my father.

'Jist Norman,' I said. Norman was the minister's son. He

was twelve, a year older than me.

'Ye don't like him, do ye?'

'He's a big snotter,' I said. 'Thinks e's great.'

'Wis he top in the bible exam as well?'

'Top equal,' I said. My father laughed.

'That minister's quite a nice wee fella,' he said. 'That time he came up here, after yer mother died, we had quite a wee chat.'

'Aye, ye told me,' I said.

'Ah think he got a surprise. Wi me no goin tae church an that, he musta thought ah was a bitty a heathen. Expected tae find me aw bitter, crackin up y'know.'

'Aye, ah know.'

'But ah wisnae. Ah showed um ma long-service badge fae the BB. Even quoted scripture at him!'

'Aye.'

' "In my father's house there are many mansions" ah said. That's the text they read at the funeral.'

'Time ah was goin,' I said.

'He wanted me tae come tae church,' said my father. 'But ah cannae be bothered wi aw that. Anywey, you're goin enough for the two ae us these days, eh?'

'Aye. Cheerio, da.'

'See ye after, son.'

I took a last look at my reflection in the squinty mirror.

'Right,' I said.

I took the shortcut to the Mission, across the back courts. It was already dark, and in the light from the windows I could make out five or six boys in the distance. From their noise I could recognize them as my friends, and I hurried on, not really wanting them to see me. If they asked where I was going, they would only mock.

I hadn't been out with them this week, except for playing

football after school. They thought I was soft in the head for going so much to the Mission. They couldn't understand. I felt a glow. It was good to feel good. It had come on stronger since my mother had died. The Mission was a refuge from the empty feeling of lack.

But part of me was always drawn back to my friends, to their rampaging and their madness.

I heard a midden-bin being overturned, a bottle being smashed, and the gang of boys scattered laughing through the backs as somebody shouted after them from a third-storey window. Head down, I hurried through a close and out into the street.

Now that I was almost at the Mission, I felt nervous and a little afraid. I had never been to an adult meeting before. I thought of the lapel-badge with the gold letters. CE. Perhaps I would even be given one tonight. Initiated. There was another badge I had seen the teachers wearing. It was green with a gold lamp, an oil lamp like Aladdin's. But maybe that was only for ministers and teachers.

Give me oil in my lamp, keep me burning.
Give me oil in my lamp I pray,
Halleluja!

The Mission hall was an old converted shop, the windows covered over with corrugated iron. A handwritten sign on the door read CHRISTIAN ENDEAVOUR. Tonight. 7.30. I stood for a moment, hesitating, outside. Then I pushed open the door and went in to the brightness and warmth.

I was early, and only a handful of people had arrived. They sat, talking, in a group near the front of the hall, and nobody seemed to have noticed me come in.

Norman was busy stacking hymn-books. Looking up, he saw me and nodded, then went out into the back room.

The minister saw me then and waved me over. There were two or three earnest conversations going on. The minister

47

introduced me to a middle-aged African couple.

'These are our very special guests,' he said. 'Mr and Mrs Lutula.'

'How do you do,' we all said, and very formally shook hands. There was a momentary lull then the conversations picked up again. But I could feel the big black woman looking at me.

'And tell me,' she said, her voice deep like a man's, 'when did the Lord Jesus come into your heart?'

'Pardon?' I said, terrified.

'Ah said, when did the Lord Jesus come into your heart, child?'

That was what I thought she had said. And she wanted an answer. From me. I looked up at the broad face smiling at me, the dark eyes shining. I looked down at the floor. I could feel myself blush. What kind of question was that to ask? How was I supposed to answer it?'

Why didn't she ask me something straightforward?

Who carried Christ's cross on the way to Calvary?

Joseph of Aramathea.

Into what estate did the fall bring mankind?

The fall brought mankind into an estate of sin and misery.

I sat, tense and rigid, on the hard wooden seat. Now my face was really hot and flushed. I cleared my throat. In a squeak of a voice I said, 'I don't know if . . .'

I looked at the floor.

She leaned over and patted my arm. 'Bless you, child,' she said, smiling, and turned to talk to her husband.

I stood up, still looking at the floor. I made my way, conscious of every step, clumsy and awkward, to the back of the hall and out into the street. I walked faster; I began to run, away from the Mission, along the street, through the close into the back court.

The night air cooled me. I stopped and leaned against a midden wall. I was in absolute misery, tortured by my own sense of foolishness. It wasn't just the question, it was what it had opened up; a realm where I knew nothing, could say nothing.

When did the Lord Jesus come into my heart? I could have said it was when my mother died. That would have sounded pious. But I didn't think it was true. I didn't know. That was it; I didn't know. If the Lord Jesus had come into my heart, I should know.

And how could I go back in now? It was all too much for me. I would tell the minister on Sunday I had felt hot and flushed, had gone outside for some air. That much was true. I would say I had felt sick and gone home.

The back court was quiet. There was no sound, except for the TV from this house or that. Bright lit windows in the dark tenement blocks. I walked on, slow, across the back, and as I passed another midden, I kicked over a bin, and ran.

Nearer home I slowed down again.

My father would ask why I was back so early.

AT MAESTRO'S

Una Flett

As a temple to Terpsichore Maestro's studio left much to be desired. It was long and narrow and dark, and the grime of London was encrusted thick upon its windows, while in the minute dressing-rooms the smell of sweat was so strong it would not have been surprising if one day it had condensed into a fine rainfall and added itself to the rivulets which ran down our bodies daily after class.

To reach it you climbed two flights of stairs past office premises that were permanently closed, and went through a door painted a vicious fading green. If you did not already know that this was Maestro's studio you would never have found out. There was no name plate, not even a card. For Maestro, unlike other ballet teachers, held himself aloof from the market place. Being proud and touchy and angrily sensitive as only a Slav can be, he expected the world to come to him as it had always done when he danced in the capitals of Europe. And if it didn't, then that was the world's loss.

It did come, in a thin trickle – a few of us drawn by the charisma of his talent and undeterred by the depressing squalor of the surroundings. For myself, sixteen years old and still concussed by the pure beauty of ballet, I hardly noticed it. The flaking paint, the lumps in the linoleum which threw you off balance, the ghastly chill of the dressing-room and the clanking sound of the lavatory unwillingly flushing out the cracked bowl – it is only in retrospect that these details stand out. At the time they were unimportant.

Then, it was not the old garments left to rot on pegs or the litter of downtrodden ballet shoes kicked under the bench

50

that made up my picture of the dressing-room. It was a place vibrant with expectation where you prepared yourself with tense anticipation for the excitement of class, the daily testing ground of your dreams, and where you recovered, gasping, at the end of the morning's work – relaxed and expansive if matters had gone well, subdued and silent if they had not.

The studio was not a place for making friendchips. We came and went, absorbed in ourselves and uninterested in each other, except during class. There, we all watched each other like hawks, jealously measuring progress against each other, jockeying for position with the height of our arabesques, the length of time we could stand on one toe, how high we could jump, how brilliantly we could turn our pirouettes.

In actual fact none of us were very brilliant at turning pirouettes except Selina, a tall girl with a large bust who could spin like a top and left the rest of us sick with envy because she could turn thirty-two times on the spot, and so had passed one of the most awful technical tests on the way to ballerinadom. When class ended with the dreaded thirty-two turns, the rest of us would be scattered in disarray while Selina, nostrils flaring, whipped round and round scattering kirby-grips and bandeaux. And when she had finished Maestro would shout 'Bravo!' and give her a kiss and, ignoring the rest of us completely, draw her aside for a private chat, the most coveted sign of favour.

'Maestro's always had a thing about big girls,' said Jackie when we were changing in the dressing-room after one of Selina's triumphs. Like the rest of us, she would infinitely prefer to accept defeat as a woman than a dancer.

'Yes,' she went on, peeling down her leotard and exposing a flat white torso quite innocent of breasts. 'It's part of his little man complex. He always goes for women who have to stoop to kiss him. Especially if they've got – ' she

51

made an eloquent cupping movement in front of her chest.

Jackie was a pert Cockney, usually good-humoured, and the nearest thing I had to a friend in the dance world. She was several years older than me and although she made fun of my accent and the fact that I 'talked like a book', she was amiable enough in a patronizing sort of way. We used to lunch together and she could tell me the gossip and show off a bit and drop names, which made us both feel good. But Selina's pirouettes had been too much for her. She swept out of the dressing-room with a brusque 'See you tomorrow', leaving us to our private reflections.

It was true that Maestro liked his big girls but he liked his little girls too. I couldn't do thirty-two turns on the spot, to my sorrow, but I had pretty legs and worked diligently and he sometimes thought it worthwhile to linger over me, positioning my arms and hands and even my smile, moulding it all into the ethereal consumptive simper of an old-style ballerina, at which times I felt that I had at least glimpsed heaven.

But most of the time it was drilling – hard, monotonous stuff like army recruits being toughened up, with legs and feet going like metronomes in the steady thump and shuffle of barre-work. Though the hands, of course, must always be held with a sort of prinking gracefulness, the head erect, the expression striving against all the odds to convey an inner state of vacuous serenity.

Maestro's following was mostly female, but on the outer fringes of our adoring coterie were various incidental males – a hefty youth with over-developed thighs, a handsome Balinese dancer who seemed always to be in silhouette, a wiry virtuoso from one of the main ballet companies who worked silently and with an air of disdain for everything going on around him.

And just occasionally, the whole class was lifted dramatically into a new and fabulous dimension by a visit from

Malenkova – slim and dark and beautiful, an international ballerina who flitted round the world giving guest performances and who, rejecting the smelly horrors of our dressing-room, changed in a corner of the main studio, nonchalantly shedding furs and scarves and jewellery until she emerged like a young knight ready for battle in the smooth armour of her perfect silk-covered muscles. She knew Maestro from his own days of stardom in the Ballets Russes when she had been a dusky prodigy in the corps de ballet, and when she arrived in a flurry of glamour and perfume there was a great burst of excited Russian chatter and Maestro's severe slant-eyed face would become radiantly animated, and Madame Millie would take Malenkova's hand in her own bony little paw with its load of junky rings and say a few words in execrable Russian, determined not to be left out.

Madame Millie? Who is Madame Millie? I should have introduced her right away. She would have expected it – indeed she would have taken matters into her own hands and barged in without waiting to be asked, as she always did at the hint of a new audience. I owe her an apology, for although she is only the class pianist, she is actually a far more significant character than Malenkova, who is merely a passing bird of paradise. But of course she has been there the whole time, as immutable a part of the scene as the practice barres or Maestro himself, banging out her terrible accompaniments, swivelling round to see what was going on, loudly correcting Maestro's reminiscences and generally making sure that no one forgot about her.

For a class pianist this was, to put it mildly, unusual. Class pianists are not normally assertive; they are expected to be biddable and tireless like a poor relative in a Victorian household, and no one wants anything from them except a reliable supply of tuneful energetic music.

But Madame Millie was not like that. She neither kept quiet nor kept good time. Nor did she let more than a day or at most two go past without a display of temperament over something. So why she was not only tolerated but allowed to get away with this outrageous behaviour, why Maestro, who might be vain and sometimes vicious but was, above all, a man of rare artistry, put up with her dreadful playing day after day was something of a mystery. It was Jackie, as always, who filled me in on the details. Madame Millie, it turned out, had also been a dancer in the Ballets Russes (corps de ballet and mime parts) and not only that, but she had been Maestro's mistress.

'You must be joking!' I said when Jackie told me.

'Not a bit of it. They were together for years. They still are, in a manner of speaking.'

I didn't stop to ask what she meant by 'a manner of speaking'. It took me a day or two to get used to the basic idea, and not for reasons of prudery. Maestro was still lithe and handsome whereas Madame Millie was an ageing figure of fun. There were her hats – straw bonnets or picture hats, all in a state of cracking decay and loaded with artificial fruit and veiling. There was her hair, still dressed in clusters of cork-screw curls despite the forbidding iron-grey of its colour. There was her make-up – especially that enormous sweetheart smile in carmine two, painted halfway across her crumpled little face. There was her fearful intensity about her music.

'I feel it *here*,' she would say, placing one hand in a flowery gesture across her bosom. 'It's the spirit of the ballet, dear – you can hear it in my music.'

You could – though it was under severe strain, for Madame Millie's idea of harmony had never progressed beyond a C major chord, and her melodies, starting out bravely with a recognizable tune, had a way of petering out into improvised nothings by about bar twelve. But there is a kind of inspiration which is almost independent of talent. In spite of the really shocking noises she made, it came through – a fusty flavour of excitement and the live theatre, footlights, gaping dark, suspense, applause and all.

Yet for all her gallantry, poor Madame Millie (whose stage name was Ludmilla Petrova and whose real name was Millicent Paterson) was part of the general run-down seediness of the place, the background of dim unaesthetic dinge against which, in splendid contrast, Maestro promenaded. Like a peacock? No, not at all – more like a perfect little English gentleman, so perfect, so beautifully laundered and cologne-scented, that he outdid any Englishman that has ever walked into a Piccadilly club. For, astonishingly, this was the disguise that fiery little Igor Ouspensky, setting aside the Tartar warriors and oriental slaves and Harlequins of his past, had chosen for his retirement.

Beside him Madame Millie looked like a crumpled paper flower, a party decoration that has seen better days. Beside the dotty extravagances of her outfits, his three-piece suits and his immaculate shirts neatly punctuated with gold at the cuffs were almost insultingly correct. No wonder I had my problems with the idea that they were, or ever had been, lovers – though if I had been older I would have known that the continuous bickering and sparring which accompanied class could only be the product of long years of intimacy. And that the terrible rows which occasionally flared up were too sore not to be rooted in some fearful matter of old scores to be settled. On these occasions, when Madame's rage was roused to the point where a genuine thick red flush burnt through the rouge of her cheeks, it was clear that Maestro – Maestro whose own temper could make your hair lift – was scared. He would start to bluster and back down; and once, when he'd told her to go to hell and she'd wound up to a swift crescendo in fluent bad French (her favourite language of abuse) – once he actually put his hand timidly on her shoulder to try to calm her down. It was the only time I'd ever seen him touch her.

That day, Jackie and I went off to have lunch together. The thundery atmosphere in class had had its effect on all of us, and I was particularly irritable for I had a feeling from dressing-room chatter that I was in the dark about matters of which everyone else was fully aware.

Over our coffee and rolls I tried to get it out of Jackie and she, as usual, started by being enigmatic.

'Why does Madame get into these terrible states?' I asked.

'Oh, it's the usual thing,' she said with a shrug. 'She's ever so touchy, and if she reckons Maestro's gone over the score she casts it all up at him.'

'Casts what up at him?'

She stared at me. 'D'you mean to say you don't know?'

I shook my head and waited as patiently as I could, while Jackie rolled her eyes and gave her usual indications that I was a hopeless case.

'Of course, you weren't around at the time, come to think of it,' she said, relenting. 'You're too young. Well, it's an old story now. He jilted her. Went off and married a nice widow lady behind her back. It must be about three years ago. They live out at Surbiton – he's got a nice little place. I've been there once for tea.' Jackie looked at me to make sure I was properly impressed by the fact that she had been invited to Maestro's home.

But I was too stunned to react. Maestro married! Living in Surbiton! It was grotesque, unbelievable. To the extent that I'd thought about the matter at all I'd imagined him and Madame Millie disappearing back into some hazy enclave of exiled Russians and other colourful folk – musicians, poets, actors. Never, never, had I considered the possibility of nice widow ladies or the scenes this conjured up – Maestro in carpet slippers, or an old cardigan and shapeless flannels mowing the lawn, neighbours, tea-drinking, a nice little place. Though I suppose those natty suits, which I'd always thought were a sort of practical joke, should have given me some inkling.

I dismissed the thought. He'd cheated – sold out on the spirit of the ballet and gone for fleshpots of the meek obedient bourgeoisie, my own boring background of bank employees and civil servants. And all this time we'd hung on his words, drunk in his inspiration, looked on him as a prophet! I was furious, with the particular fury that comes from knowing that you have eagerly contributed to your own duping.

As for Madame Millie, no wonder she shook and trembled so easily with rage! No wonder that Maestro was scared and backed down when the simmerings of an ever-present betrayal threatened to get out of hand. But, when you came to think of it, the really surprising thing was that Madame Millie should still be on the scene at all.

'How is it that Madame still comes to the studio?' I asked. 'After all that?'

'Well,' said Jackie thoughtfully, 'she's not the sort of woman to let a little thing like a wife get in her way – not after fifteen years with Maestro. She said she had her "rights" and she was going to stick by them. When he tried to stop her playing for class she accused him of wanting her to starve. He told her he couldn't take her to the ballet any more – and she used to turn up to every first night dressed up to the nines and make a scene in front of everybody, until he got so scared he agreed that she could come too. And now they get invited everywhere together, the three of them. I don't know what Mrs makes of it.' She laughed. 'I feel sorry for Maestro sometimes. She's got him by the short and curlies, hasn't she?'

We finished our coffee in silence. 'Time I was off,' said Jackie. 'See you tomorrow.'

She disappeared into the busy London street, vanishing into her own life and leaving me to mine. We knew nothing of each other's existence outside class, which was the way it should be. Knowing about people meant that you were left with half-finished stories to puzzle and worry away at. Like Madame Millie – where did she go, what did she do when Maestro went home to Surbiton? What was there for her to do, outside the studio, except stoke the fires of her grievances and plan her costume for the next day? For her there was nothing, except the fading spirit of the ballet. I started to feel depressed. I imagined her sitting over her boxes of jewellery, trying on one trashy trinket after another, looking at herself searchingly in the mirror the way she did in class between exercises. I saw her rummaging in cases and cupboards, thinking, planning, preparing herself. I thought of her grim little mouth embedded in all that greasepaint, the way she stared with a sort of crazed fixity from under the brim of one of her absurd hats, and it seemed as if the beauty and glitter of the ballet was being replaced by something hopeless and sad.

It was not so many weeks later that I decided I'd had enough of Maestro's place. The feeling of times past which had so fascinated me, the reminiscences, the reliving of former glories, even Maestro's brilliant little snatches of dance, all started to have a flavour of mouldy stagnation. I got wind of other teachers, the possibility of auditions, gossip about forthcoming shows in which dancers would be needed. It all seemed to be happening elsewhere. So one day I sneaked off, feeling too mean even to say goodbye or thank you. And instead I went to studios where ashen-faced teachers taught from morning till night, and the pianos were banged efficiently by people I'd never recognize again, and we worked and worked and worked, and the spirit of the ballet turned out to be mainly a matter of mortifying the flesh.

PLATFORM TICKET

Robert A. Crampsey

The early afternoon sun slanted fiercely through the windows
of the Glasgow Corporation Transport School attached to
Newlands Tram Depot. It was late May, the trees in full leaf,
no day for school even when school was a concrete hut. The
small room had eighteen wooden chairs, arranged in twos the
length of the room with a passageway between each pair. On
one wall was a huge map of the City of Glasgow, on another
photographs of the Seven Ages of the Tramcar. These
started with the horse-drawn vehicles of the nineties and
progressed through the various developments which had
culminated in the apotheosis of the tramcar, the Coronation
model of 1937, still touchingly referred to in this year of 1952
as the 'new' tram.

The small room had also eighteen trainee conductors, one
per wooden chair. Between the feet of each conductor lay a
leather money-satchel and a metal ticket machine, the latter
very modern with windows which displayed the numbers of
the ticket rolls.

Archie Fleming, one of three university students in the
room, shifted uncomfortably on his chair as the short, red-
haired Transport Inspector, name of Laurie but known to his
underlings as Rob Roy, prepared to deliver his afternoon
homily to the conductors-to-be.

Pity that Joan got engaged to the languages student,
Fleming reflected. The plain secretary of the Students'
Representative Council, she had taken a fancy to Archie,
helped on by his natural politeness, and had put several
plum vacation jobs in his way. He thought ruefully of the

59

idyllic week spent showing the US Navy midshipmen from Annapolis over such typical Scottish scenes as Gleneagles and Turnberry. He thought, even more ruefully, of the fortnight spent as guide-chauffeur to the attractive, fortyish American widow. She had been interested enough in the Aberdeen-shire countryside but, being very much a disciple of Pope, had had no difficulty in believing that the proper study of mankind was man.

Well, Joan was engaged, no help for it, the future plums were for the languages student. If the trams weren't exhilar-ating, they were a better vacation prospect than the legendary dye-works, where students laboured in a steamy heat for very little. Rob Roy's words began to shape themselves in his mind.

'This school was set up by the Transport Manager, Earl Fitzpayne – he's not a nobleman, those are his initials, E.R.L. – to provide a quick course for tram and bus conductors. I almost said a crash course, but that might have been an un-fortunate choice of phrase.'

The lecturer spoke in an expressionless mutter. Two years later, Fleming would have recognized the delivery as NCO Instructor Mark I, but now it had all the charm of novelty. He fixed the Inspector with an interested, loyal look.

'You will not merely be conducting a tramcar or motorbus,' Rob Roy told his apathetic audience of students, unemploy-ables, Sikh immigrants and Irishmen. 'You are selling trans-port. You must make passengers want to travel on YOUR vehicle.' Fleming was soon to discover that the art of con-ducting was the exact antithesis of this.

'Be courteous to the public, but firm,' droned the Inspector. 'If you have a schedule, stick to it. You could take a tram up to Rouken Glen today and if you kept it there till Christmas Eve, some old wife would come running after it as you eventually started off.' His mouth fell sideways slightly as he said this, sufficient evidence that it was intended as light relief. Three sycophants laughed obligingly.

Some more information was provided on who could legally travel on a tramcar without paying. Renfrewshire policemen in uniform could, but not the Lanarkshire constabulary – or perhaps it was the other way round, the afternoon was warm and Archie had slightly lost Rob Roy. Suddenly the room sprang to life and the purpose of the odd seating arrangements became apparent. The trainees donned their machines and satchels and pretended to sell each other tickets, a task which noticeably strained the arithmetical powers of Belfast and Lahore. One African, however, with tribal markings which spoke of Ashanti, mastered with amazing rapidity the art of returning the minimum of change in the maximum of coins. Half an hour of this and Rob Roy expressed himself as reasonably pleased.

'You're coming, aye, you're coming. Sell your product. You'll have three days in the school here, four days on the job with an experienced conductor, then you'll be ready to go solo. Return machines and satchels, and that'll do for today.'

Four days later, in light green linen dust jacket, heavy serge green trousers and peaked cap, Archie learned the real conductor's art from his mentor, Davie Willocks. Scruffy, pimply, his straight black hair escaping in spikes from beneath his cap, Willocks's small frame heaved with mingled indignation and scornful dismissal as Archie recounted his lessons of the transport school.

The first journey of the day had been made and the car was stopped in the terminus for a few minutes before beginning the return trip. Already Archie had admired the deft way in which Davie had changed the trolley over and lit a Woodbine in almost the same movement.

'Who was it instructed ye? Oh! Laurie! [This from Archie's vague description of him.] Ye'll learn bugger all from that idiot!'

Willocks, wizened in a peculiar, youthful way, black tie gaping in a Windsor knot as big as a bolster, weirdly contrasting with the immaculate white shirt and neat tie of the ex-miner driver, Andy Beaton, cursed richly when told of the 'selling transport' line of approach.

'It's no' right to mislead lads with that rubbish. Listen, the whole thing in this game is to carry as few people as possible. He's talkin' of sellin' transport, but you or me will no' be bloody well paid by results. You watch the drivers ye get. A good one will get to a school five minutes after the weans go in or ten after they get out. At a crossroads where two cars have to go the same way – ye'll have seen them hold up their fingers to each other?'

Archie nodded. 'It's times, isn't it?'

Willocks looked at him. 'Well, they're no imitatin' Churchill. The good driver'll always go second, and the fella in front will be slaughtered.'

'You mean, a driver'd tell lies about his times?'

'Terrible, i'ntit? If Ah draw a week's duty wi' someone who doesny, the conductor-murderers we call them, Ah go sick. He wouldny say anything to you about hats?'

'Who?'

'Laurie!'

A headshake. 'Only that we should be smartly dressed at all times.'

'Look, the only part of yer uniform that matters a curdie is yer hat, only it mustny be YOUR hat.'

Archie looked at him, puzzled. 'Sorry, Davie, I'm not quite with you.'

'Yer a student, aren't ye?'

'Yes, Geography. I'll teach after my National Service. I've got a day off in June to graduate.'

'Ah suppose they'll give ye a commission?'

'I can try for one once I go into the RAF.'

'Let's hope yer quicker in the uptake about hats there.

Look, every day before ye take a tram out, change hats wi'
another conductor. Then, when ye have an argument wi' a
passenger, and ye will – especially on the Number Three,
that's Mosspark–University, and it's crawling wi' snooty auld
bitches – ye refuse to gie yer name. "That's all right," she'll
say, "I'll just take yer number and report ye to Bath Street."
"Go ahead, madam," says you, and then when the complaint
comes in and yer carpeted, ye simply say that the poor lady
has got the wrong number, and if they like to check, they'll
see that ye were on another tram that day. And there's an end
of that.'

'How did you work all this out, Davie?'

'Experience, and common sense. What did Laurie say
about drunks?'

'He didn't mention them especially. Always be polite to
your customers was about the strength of it.'

'That'll do ye bugger all good on a Glasgow tram on a
Friday or Saturday night. Or any night. It's amazing the
bears that can get steamboats even on a Sunday. Listen,
Archie, the great thing is never to let a drunk on if ye can
help it. Always stay downstairs near the platform coming
through the town. If it's a new car, ye've the driver's cabin
either end. Reach in, grab the points-changer, reverse it, and
if the drunk still shows signs of coming on, let him have it in
the crotch. Then give yer driver four bells and away like the
clappers. It's sinful no' to tell ye these things. Wan other
thing, Archie, don't fiddle the cash.'

'I haven't the slightest . . .'

'Never knew a student yet who didn't try. The skin's fair
enough, but don't overdo it. Don't tell me ye've never . . . ?'
His question trailed off in the face of Fleming's headshake.
With weary patience, the conductor explained matters to this
young academic innocent.

'Look, it's fair game to skin the price of twenty fags from
each half of yer shift.'

'You could never get away with that, Davie.' As he spoke, Fleming had an uneasy feeling that already he was more interested in the mechanics than the morality of the exercise.

'Could ye no'? Ye take a tram in from Shawlands to Argyle Street in the morning rush hour and see how much time ye'll have to collect yer top deck. When it comes to Jamaica Street, ye'll have about twenty folks piling downstairs with their fares in their hands.'

'But you'd have to give them a ticket surely?'

'Granted, but not necessarily the one they ask for. If they want a fourpenny one, give them their change, if any, and ring up a tuppence-ha'penny ticket. They're no' wanting a ticket or watching as they jump off the car, just throw the ticket on the floor. Surely to God ye can work out how often ye've to do that to make twenty fags.'

He stood up. 'School's over, time you bloody learned the facts of life.'

In the weeks and months that followed, Archie saw that Willocks's plan was perfectly feasible in the rush hour. He began to look closely at conductors when he himself was travelling as a passenger, but could detect no impropriety. Indeed the only departure he noticed was when a very smartly turned out and ladylike conductress followed an old man off the car to give him the change which he'd forgotten to collect.

All down the summer, Archie developed his conducting skills and, precisely because they were little skills, he cherished them. Hamfisted by nature, he was absurdly proud when he could load his ticket machine dexterously. He learned to welcome pound notes towards the end of a shift. It made paying-in easier and lightened the weight of the satchel. Four hours of toting that and the ticket machine caused a dull ache in the shoulders and the vee of the groin. He acquired the knack of spotting an Irish coin half a mile off on a foggy day, and many Glaswegians appeared to have travelled exclusively in the Republic in time past. He coped with belligerent football fans, shopping women who were fumbling and slow, and children who, returning from Rouken Glen or Hogganfield Loch, drenched the floor with their ill-digested picnics from one orifice or another. He learned that there was more than one use for the sandbox.

He began to think like the conductors, and grew to dislike the Gestapo, as the mobile disciplinary force of inspectors was called. They cruised around in unobtrusive little green vans, and kept watch for drivers who smoked, drivers who arrived at check points late – or early, drivers who allowed their student conductors to drive the trams on the private section of track at Speirsbridge. The Gestapo, strangely enough, were also death to those transport salesmen who removed the stiffeners from their hats, thereby giving them a raffish, German High Command appearance.

Archie fell foul of them for an incomplete waybill and, more seriously, when on two consecutive mornings he failed to make the 4.17 a.m. car which took early workers to the shipyards in Clydebank. For this, he was awarded a week on the 'Yellow Peril', Number Seven, the toughest tram route in Glasgow, which meandered through Govan, Gorbals and Bridgeton. If there was any especially tough street, the Number Seven route would make a detour to include it, and it finished, with an instinctive sense of artistry, beneath the walls of Barlinnie Prison.

Archie would never have put the skin successfully to the test but for Senga. They had first met when they shared a spare shift one languorously warm Sunday afternoon. A spare shift was a pleasant chore – it meant sitting in the canteen until a call came for a conductor to replace someone who'd gone sick or failed to turn up. If no call came before half the shift was over, the supervisor often let you go off a couple of hours early. Senga was the only other spare that day and she and Archie had the canteen entirely to themselves as they sat in the small room off the main hall. She was a nicely-built little girl who would have been very pretty but for a slight yet noticeable squint (Archie's mother would have called it a Norma Shearer glee). She moved up very close to Archie, who for politeness had to lower his paper.

'Ah like it in the summer when the students are here. They're right devils, so they are.' She laughed happily.

Archie, sensible that a compliment was intended, muttered a deprecatory phrase.

'Your name's Archie, sure it is? I heard Big Annie call you that the other morning when your roll on sausage was ready. Ye've got lovely wavy hair, but it should be fairer. With your very blue eyes, you should definitely have fairer hair.'

Archie, sorry to disappoint a lady, was totally unprepared for what came next.

'Ah fancy you. Huz anybody ever told you you've got lovely thighs?'

With perfect truth, Archie said he was learning this for the first time. Senga, deed following words, placed both her hands on Archie's thighs and began to knead them vigorously. Suddenly she pulled him down towards her by slipping a hand inside his jacket. As he stumbled over Senga and the wooden bench, a bell rang in the empty, sunny, dust-dancing room, the signal for a spare. Archie disentwined himself from the clutching, moaning Senga, but not before the duty roster man had come along to see if there was in fact anyone on call. The student reputation for devilry had been enhanced.

And, Archie thought, since it had, since in a month he was off on holiday before his year at teacher training college, why not ask Senga out? He had been encouraged to think she might come, by one or two hints she had just dropped, and there was no danger of a long-term entanglement. He handed over all his wages bar thirty shillings to his parents every week, but perhaps now was the time to test the Willocks Theory.

It worked, even as Willocks had said it would. At the end of the week, Archie, who'd been keeping a close check, calculated that he had siphoned off forty-one shillings which, being a non-smoker, he proposed to spend on Senga. In the Golden Divans at Green's Playhouse and after, she showed herself to be athletic, pneumatic and great fun.

Stick to rush hour, morning or evening, although morning's better, don't get greedy. In the next two weeks, he and Senga spent all their off-duty time together. Archie liked her enormously, although her habit of finishing every other sentence with, 'Sure it is?', 'Isn't it not?', would in time have proved tedious. The beauty about the skin was that the conductor really HAD to hover about the platform, otherwise passengers poured on and overloaded the car.

At the start of his last week, Archie had been assigned a morning shift, one of the very few that involved an eight till five day. Such shifts were highly prized and he knew that he had Laurie to thank for it, as he, amongst other tasks, was involved with the duty rosters.

The Tuesday morning was bitterly cold for mid-August, with slanting, cutting rain. Umbrellas were an additional hazard in the crowded, sodden tram, and the usual discipline of the tram queues buckled under the icy lash of the squalls. By Newlands Road the tram was full, and from then on, by Shawlands Cross, Allison Street, Eglinton Toll and Bridge Street, Archie's total energies were directed to keeping the number of standing passengers to a minimum. Buffeted, and Canute-like, he compromised by allowing eight, three more than he had to, and about ten less than popular demand would have inflicted. Half a dozen men dotted about the lower deck of the tram read their *Heralds* resolutely as they'd been doing since Giffnock, diligently avoiding any feminine eye which might look mutely reproachful.

Even on such a day, Argyle Street was reached at last. The tram emptied like water from a bath, a stampede of the young and fit from the smoky top deck, the slower withdrawal of the more staid from the lower. The platform whirled and eddied with humanity as Archie took money, gave change, rang up tickets and threw them on the floor.

'Just a minute, conductor.' A hand on his sleeve. The two businessmen who had been sitting on either side of the gangway had risen and now, as the platform cleared, they stepped on to it. One showed a card. Archie managed an impassive expression, but knew he had been unable to control his colour. The taller man spoke quietly, conversationally. He informed Archie of what they had seen from close quarters. An inspector and relief conductor would join the tram two stops on at the Transport Offices. The relief conductor would not know why he was taking over, the Inspector would take care of Archie's satchel and, of course, the ticket machine. It was to be hoped that he would not do anything which might hold up the tram, people after all had to get to business.

It had, of course, been too good a story to be passed up by the papers. Archie's bag had been found to contain 7/9d more than the value of the tickets issued; an error of that magnitude could not be explained away so early in a shift. Over the last two years, the Transport Department had been concerned that increased fares had brought in the same revenue, although passengers carried had also increased.

The reaction was predictably severe. 'Student Flayed for Breach of Trust', said the small but all too huge headline in the *Evening News*. The *Evening Citizen* led with 'Student Blights Career for 7/9d', and the *Evening Times*, in sardonic vein, 'Student Fails to Save His Skin'. The case and its disclosures had left Archie shaken and ill. There was the horror of his family and the sorrow of his friends; there was the letter from the Training College regretting that it found itself unable to offer him the place which he had been about to take up. There had been another subsequent letter from the RAF stating as there was reason to believe that he would not be continuing as a full-time student, his deferment was at an end. He should report to RAF Padgate for initial training. The letter did not formally state that he was now ineligible for a commission, but there was no need.

The court had stated that serious consideration had been given to the imposition of a prison sentence, but it was felt that a heavy fine, because of the peculiar disgrace attaching, would be a sufficiently punitive sentence. The public was entitled to a modicum of basic honesty from those on whom it had lavished time and money for their higher education. The papers received several letters from people who said that if this was how students behaved, they thanked God they were only factory hands/mill girls/roadmen. Hardest to bear had been the look of puzzled, cold contempt which Laurie had directed at him in court when the case was held.

Archie had asked that no one come with him when he went for the Manchester train which would bear him off to the RAF. He sat quietly in the corner of a full compartment as they clacked slowly out over the Central Station bridge towards Eglinton Street. Almost immediately they stopped for a signal. Archie, idly glancing out, saw a tram – it was red so it was an Eight, a Twenty-five or a Fourteen – trundling down Eglinton Street, empty, since it was mid-morning. The conductor stood on the platform, lounging against the rail, cigarette in mouth. He looked a bit like Willocks, or at least the stance did, but as the train and tram picked up speed and sped in divergent directions, it was difficult to be sure.

THE STATE OF THE NATION
AND OTHER MYTHOLOGIES

Campbell Black

'In the course of his duties as Lecturer in Scottish History at the University of Glasgow, Dr J. S. McTaggart went entirely insane and was frequently seen indulging himself in irrational conversations with non-existent companions in the vicinity of Byres Road.'

– A student's unfinished novel, Glasgow, c 1960

'My dear,' said the woman as she stepped into the conservatory, where several plants had expired or were in advanced stages of rot for want of both light and water: 'My dear, are you quite well today?'

The man, huddled in a tartan travel-rug, did not move for a time; he had been observing the disintegration of his philodendron, noticing that as the plant moved towards its final decay, it assumed a shape that reminded him intermittently of both a large spider and a small crouching rodent. In truth, he was far from well, although he would not have admitted this to anyone, least of all to the woman who had just come in. She stood in the doorway in the sad manner of a retired pugilist, her fists flexed involuntarily tight, a certain small savage light in her eye.

'Would you like cocoa, my dear? Hot cocoa?'

The man watched the dying plant; he could not bring himself to contemplate cocoa for the moment. Later, perhaps, when he had cleared his mind: there was always a 'later', like a tiny boxed-off area of the future into which he shoved his various indecisions. Although not himself, he was not entirely miserable. He thought of how the dying plant would serve to nurture the dry soil in which it expired, he thought of this as being of historic significance in its own small way, as though the philodendron's death were analogous to a faded medieval document, to scribblings upon dehydrated parchment, some cosmic hieroglyph. To each thing, he thought, there is a programme, to each thing a code. And he considered tea-leaves, coffee grounds, the flaking flower of a dead dandelion, the floating vegetable matter of a cockaleekie soup.

He moved his hands beyond the fringe of his rug and flapped them as if they were wet. He heard distantly the woman's impatient sigh in the doorway and was reminded of a wind coming unwanted upon a serene landscape. He could not remember if this woman were his wife or some impostor, perhaps a nurse loaned out for a time by one or other branch of the National Health Service.

The glass-paned conservatory smelled of various things; the stale emissions of the strangled plants, the urine of cats who came in through broken windows at night in the fashion of drunks invading a public lavatory, the mustiness of his tartan rug. He stood up from his chair, reassembled himself, then sat down once again and still the woman sighed uncomfortably in the doorway.

'Perhaps a nice cup of tea?' she asked.

He was in the cave, watching the spider swing on its single shimmering strand, a minuscule acrobat quivering through the air. As he observed the insect he became conscious, through the narrow mouth of the cave, of the sea darkly beating along the shore, a sound of hammered anxiety. There is a message in all this for me, he thought: but what? and how? The spider failed again, knocking itself down from its sinewy string and falling, falling, falling, into a small cairn of rock. He sighed and shrugged and rubbed his hands together like a

miser awaiting the fruition of his investment. He looked along
the pebbled shore to the white tide. I can save the nation, he
thought; and the thought, like some celestial candle of
destiny, burned in his head.

Soon, a shadow fell across the entrance to the cave and he
found himself staring at the woman who stood there with her
long untidy hair falling over her shoulders, lank damp with
fine seaspray. She carried lilies in one hand. For a while she
said nothing to him; then, in a resigned way, asked if he were
watching spiders again. He could hardly deny this, even
though he knew that an admission would entail her terrible
wrath. Her words were always the same: Other men go out
and do an honest day's work and you just sit here watching
those damned spiders, etcetera: he closed his eyes. Somewhere, he knew, there hung a fine balance that he would find
in time. And time, wheat in the season of famine, was scarce.

'Professor Saltash is on the telephone,' she said.

He did not move but he felt that somewhere an anachron-
ism was being perpetrated. Momentarily his mind was fused,
disjointed, various connecting wires having been blown quite
away.

'Do you not want to speak with him?' she asked.

Awaiting an answer that she knew would not come, the
woman drummed her fingers upon a pane of glass and was
slightly irritated to see, imbedded upon her whorls, particles
of dust. She returned to the telephone and spoke to Professor
Saltash.

'He cannot come to the telephone,' she said, rather simply.

Professor Saltash, after years in various academies, had
grown tolerant and humane, had become quite accustomed
to the fact that his lesser colleagues succumbed to different
pressures; and was presently more interested in any case in
his application for a distinguished Oxford Chair than he was
in the Lecturer's problems, problems which, as well he knew,

would dissolve in time as did all things; and besides, he had become quite handy at perceiving the flux of things, at viewing human endeavour *sub specie aeternitatis*, and so he was not overly concerned with trivia.

'He cannot come to the telephone. He cannot come to the telephone,' said the Professor. 'He cannot come to the telephone. He cannot come to the telephone. That is all there is to this matter.'

He replaced the receiver and looked down from the window of his office along University Avenue, imagining as usual that he could hear the rattle of the Kelvin as it hurried to the Clyde. He thought for a while of tributaries, of the flow of things, of arms, legs, livers and veins, and divers appendages and organs.

'I told him,' said the woman. 'Now, if you think you will be fine for a time, I have to go out . . .'

The man in the tartan rug did not answer; he did not hear, in fact. He had his mind on something terribly disturbing.

'I have to be at a meeting of the Kelvinside Ladies' Conservative Organization where we intend to discuss fund raising for our candidate. An Englishman, I am sorry to report. We tried to find a home-grown candidate, but the only response we had was from a Clydebank Marxist wishing to run under the Tory banner, claiming that he was interested in a general synthesis of aims and goals. He argued well, but finally he was too preposterous.'

Again the man did not speak. Signs in the landscape of his mind, of which territory he was a tireless observer, had indicated that there were English forces foraging over the border, streaming in from Carlisle and through Gretna, raping Scottish girls and behaving in other uncharitable ways. They came rampaging up the M6 highway, crossbowed and intent on genocide. He closed his eyes. Rhetoric would not dissuade them; it would do no good to stand in their advance and ren-

der a line or two from Barbour, for they were Philistines uninterested and unattuned to the deeper mysteries of Celtic
verse. They did not have a mythology, which was their basic
psychological problem; they did not have a Pictish past, nor
heathery hills, nor tiny souvenir bagpipes. No: he would not
quote them verse, he would assemble his troops and meet
the enemy at a place decided upon by destiny.

The woman, stooping slightly, withdrew; saying, as she
stooped, that she would not be gone for long.

He addressed his troops. He told them of how he had observed a certain spider and of what he had learned from his
observations. He spoke at some length to his proud com-
patriots about the need to keep one's eyes open, to perceive
the comings and the goings of nature.

His captains watched him closely. His lieutenants watched
him closely. They were suspicious of anyone who eulogized a
spider. In general, they were fighting men who, when they
did not have a battle to attend, indulged in hard drinking;
and who, when drunk, looked eagerly for fresh battles. Their
lifestyles were vicious. They fingered their crossbows
anxiously while listening to the drama of the spider. He told
them that horse-drawn carts were hauling heavy English
artillery across the border; an item of information more
interesting to his men than that which concerned the spider.
They cheered when they heard of the enemy's advance.

Meanwhile, having withdrawn from both conservatory and
house, the woman took a bus to the HQ of the Conservative
Party, which was located in a National Trust house close to
the Botanic Gardens. It was late summer and there was
fragrance in the room filled with hats. Mrs Tweedie, whose
husband was a general practitioner, and whose two sons
were plastic surgeons in London no less and who spent much
of their time discussing facial renovation and grafting in the
resort of Torquay, this same Mrs Tweedie asked:

'And how is your man today?'

'I can't say,' said the woman. 'Some days are better than others. Other days are worse than some.'

'Now,' said Mrs Tweedie, eyeing the other woman's thinly lipsticked mouth; 'now, if you'll pardon a suggestion, I think your man might find a hobby to occupy himself while he . . . ahem, convalesces . . . My Hector, albeit being a busy sort of man, has his own hobby. He collects wrecked motor cars. It may sound morbid, but it's an interest for him in his spare time. Wherever there is an accident, that is where you will find Hector, haggling with representatives of insurance companies.'

The chairlady, a Mrs Bowman, called the meeting to order. All behatted heads in the big room focused upon Mr Bute's upcoming campaign, which he was certain to win; his opponents were a troublesome Trade Unionist called McNab, and a scholarly Scottish Nationalist also called McNab, and neither of these candidates was thought to have much of a chance in the Kelvinside district. The question, then, of Mr Bute's campaign was not especially taxing to the ladies in the big room.

Leaning forward, his eyes now open, he watched the ragtaggle philodendron wilt in its clay pot. Even though the surrounding hills were alive with the English forces, he thought that nevertheless there would be time for a woman before the conflict began. He found one, Bannockburn Lil, of whom it was said that she could accommodate the entire English army before breakfast and still remain dissatisfied. He took her out to a nearby hill and together they lay down in the bracken. She sang softly in his ear: *Come O'er the Stream Charlie, dear Charlie* . . . He was transported by a mixture of pride and patriotism; she called him Bob and told him that he was wonderful, just the job, and she confessed to him that those dark rumours concerning the sexual prowess of the English were absurdly unfounded. Sir John Cope might build humpbacked bridges but that was as much as *she* could find to say about him.

He rose now, dropping the tartan rag, and moved cautiously towards the plant. Beneath it, covered in an array of fallen wrinkled leaves, lay several typescripts that he recognized as his own work. One was a full-length manuscript entitled: *Did Scotland Sleep? An Account of An Illegal Union*; the other was an essay called *The Rise of Jock Stein: A history of the Celtic Football Club, Religion, Immigration and the Potato Famine*. These, although they had been offered several times to various publishers and magazines, had never seen print. They had come back with offensive regularity to him, accompanied by urbane letters written mainly in London which complained of 'structural inadequacy' or 'incomprehensibility' or informed him that his work was 'not commercially viable at this time': even as he looked at his old typescripts, he experienced a moment of extraordinary clarity in which he realized that the fault lay not with himself but with other minds; that he could not blame himself for his populist-dialectical-oral approach to history, rather that the flaw lay in others whose mentalities were so structured that they could not see the impossibility of deductive history. The clarity, such as it was here, did not last for long. He went back to his chair and drew the rug about his face and tried to sleep.

They were on the outskirts of Derby and he felt raddled after a night's hard drinking; the air smelled of goat's milk gone stale and old ale mouldering in cups and unwashed Scottish figures grown weary of their long campaign. He emerged from his tent and saw the city spread out before him. Limbs ached, his tongue was raw, several darkening spots flew flylike in front of his eyes. There was a possibility that he might sack the city; equally, he might not. Indecision dogged him, he was harried by his own befuddled moral purpose. Besides, he had heard that a number of his own men had already deserted the troops and were selling souvenirs – sprigs of heather, used sporrans, tiny souvenir bagpipes – in the streets of Derby; and that, in the best old entrepreneurial tradition, they were doing fine trade. Could he sack a city in which were ensconced his own men? He called together his captains, an unruly lot faithful to him, and in the course of this emergency council spoke to them of spiders.

Scotland is like the spider, he told them.

Derby is the fly.

We are the spider weaving a web.

Do we, or do we not, weave a web round Derby?

Do we weave Derby into our web?

Do we web our weave round Derby?

He spoke at length on the virtues of David Hume's view of causality and of how the *Sunday Post* represented all that was upright in the Scottish tradition. He talked of the lesson of Flodden, he predicted Culloden. He sang several stanzas of *Hey Johnny Cope!* in a tuneless baritone. He reminisced of the Glasgow girls he had loved, Mary Hill, Bella Houston, Ruth Erglen, Poll Okshaws and that Old Cow Caddens. He debated the wisdom of Scott giving up romantic ballads in favour of cheap novels, concluding that this would be a grave loss to our literature. He argued that McDiarmid's concept of Lallans was preposterous and fraudulent, an attempt to regurgitate the bones of a dead language at worst, a futile effort to create an artificial one at best. He likened Oor Wullie to Robert the Bruce, in the sense that both appeared to sit for great periods of time on upturned buckets. He argued the merits of George Young as Scotland's greatest postwar captain and deplored the view that this laurel should go to Billy Bremner. He talked for a time on the authenticity or otherwise of Fyffe Robertson. He claimed that George Blake's *The Shipbuilders* was a reactionary work of questionable morality. Finally, depleted, sensing that he was losing the interest of his men, he began to drink ale in quantity, as did his bored captains, and they formed a semi-circle to sing *Come O'er the Stream Charlie and Dine With McLean*. He wondered as to the identity of this McLean, but it did not matter. Nothing mattered. His drunk army left Derby at dawn. And nothing mattered. The course of history had changed. But nothing mattered. His men would be butchered on Culloden Field and the land put to flame by Wild Bill Cumberland, but there would be Flora, and Flora was the siren of the sea, the salt of the earth, and after Flora France, and inebriated exile and a roaring trade in genuine snuffboxes. On the long march north his maudlin troops sang *O We're No Awa' Tae Bide Awa'*.

He walked disjointedly to the kitchen and there brewed himself a cup of cocoa and read that day's edition of the *Daily Record*.

A cache of horrible weapons had been found in a Possilpark tenement: proud policemen were to be seen in posed photographs displaying sawn-off shotguns, dreadful razors, sharpened metal combs, grenades, and studded leather belts. The Irish Republican Army was being blamed and, by telephone, had gratefully accepted the blame. Someone had claimed that a timebomb had been placed in the Glasgow Stock Exchange: there was no such bomb. A housewife in Airdrie, Lanarkshire, had written a letter extolling the virtue of carrot-stew during a time of economic belt-tightening: 'cheap, nutritious, and Scottish to the last drop'. A curious Indian-like figure was to be seen in a strip-cartoon imbibing huge quantities of Barr's Irn-Bru. A minister in Pittenweem, Fife, was bringing in a rockband to 'jazz up' his Sunday services and to revive interest in the deity during 'the rock age'. A woman in Gatehouse-of-Fleet, Kirkcudbrightshire, was being ostracized by her neighbours for having once danced in a topless manner in a Stranraer public house.

He found all of this grey, incoherent, a trifle bleak: what did it all add up to? He could think only of some fine thread of lunacy being woven in the atmosphere all around him, a shift in the cosmos. It made no sense: it sold newspapers, but it made no sense. The *Daily Record* made no sense. The world made no sense. Glasgow made no sense. Only a few days ago, while he had been walking across Kelvingrove Park and had been about to step upon the Prince of Wales Bridge, he had been ruthlessly accosted by several students in their black and gold scarves who had invited him to submit his brain after death (or before, they joked, it made no difference to them) to science. They wanted his cadaver, his head. Wrapping his face in his own black and gold scarf he had stumblingly hurried away. No sense, do you see? The philodendron was dying: no sense.

Carrying his cocoa, spilling it with a little trembling, he went back to the conservatory and out through a rear door to a small walled yard. It was one of those hazy misty obscure Glasgow days in which all things seem destined to perish, in which nothing has any great definition. He listened for birds, he heard the squabbling of sparrows. And somewhere the sound, the shrill, of a telephone ringing.

He did not answer it.

He would not answer it for there was always the chance that it would be the young woman who, under the pretext of offering one free dancing lesson at McBride's Palais de Danse on the Gallowgate, was in fact attempting to purvey subscriptions to the Scottish Freedom Movement whose members, so she claimed, consisted of retired Teddyboys, lapsed priests and agitated old colonels made apoplectic by the disintegration of their fine regiments.

So, fearing a further confrontation with this voice, he did not answer the ringing; which, after a few moments, stopped in any case.

Mrs Tweedie, who had an ear for the solicitous phrase, the well-lathed platitude, the finely-soldered word of solace, addressed a group of other women in the coffee lounge of an hotel in Bath Street: 'We should feel sorry, ladies, we should try to alleviate the burdens of our colleagues. Her man is plainly . . . mad. More's the pity. But she is a good Conservative and we must do our bit.'

Or fall for the flag if we must: someone might have added this, but the timbre of the company was quite wrong.

Appalled, his eye fell upon a copy of the *Francis Gay Friendship Book*, even as he wondered whether the English might have been responsible for the removal of tramcars from the city; and there seemed some rather curious linkage in his head between the absence of the old trams and the *Friendship Book*, as if both were symptoms of a similar malady. It would not be beneath the English to dismantle the tramcar system: their avaricious imperialistic attitudes were all too evident, wherever he looked; and besides, his experience of fighting wars against them had taught him that they were not exactly trustworthy. He had enjoyed riding the trams, after all. He had ridden the whole complex in his time, Millerston to Rouken Glen, Riddrie to Giffnock, he had been shaken by riding the front upstairs compartment all the way from Shettleston to Duke Street to the London Road and down by the murkier pastures of Glasgow Green . . . But there were no tramcars now; and diesels did not have quite the panache of the older mode of transport. But could he squarely blame the English for their absence?

Yes, he could.

But wasn't it irrational?

No, of course not.

Was it not fair exchange that in return for the trams we received Polaris bases?

No. The Polaris missiles were no substitute. They did not cover the same routes. QED.

Do you blame the English for
everything?   They are an imperfect race and
        ipso facto highly blameworthy.
Are you saying then that Jane
Austen could not have written
Dr Jekyll?   My point is taken, sir.

Feeling a new infusion of the old and gorgeous anglo-
phobia, he pulled his rug about his shoulders and sipped his,
by now, cold cocoa. The English, he speculated, were a
parcel of rogues. Had they not in their time attempted to
deplete the motherland's supply of pipers by throwing such
instrumentalists into the front lines of military engagements?
And, following this luminous thread of contemplation, were
there not other conspiracies afoot? Was it not the case that
several factories in Yorkshire were being retooled for the
purpose of producing counterfeit souvenirs, such as tiny
bagpipes and sprigs of plastic heather? Could it be the case
that his beloved Edinburgh Rock was manufactured in
Slough? Could it not further be assumed that such manifestly
Scottish personalities as . . . for the sake of argument,
Clifford Hanley . . . were manufactured in London studios
and sent north, complete with beard and accent, to infiltrate
Old Scotia? The endlessness of such speculation wearied him
enormously; and he felt the blight of a brief sadness settle
upon him.

Perhaps Knox had been right: perhaps, during their last
conversation, Knox had been correct when he had argued the
case for an ethnic religion supervised by a God who was truly
Scottish; a Scottish God whom Knox had defined as having
the usual attributes of your ordinary deity – including omni-
science, omnipotence, omnipresence – but who had also the
qualities of the Scotsman, qualities Knox perceived as
diligence, thrift, humility, and a working knowledge of the
streets of Aberdeen.

They had argued thus:

How could a God be both God and a Scotsman?

Dead easy that, Knox had said. No special theological fankle in that.

But how can he be omnipotent and still be defined under such a narrow secular concept as diligence, let us say?

Listen, Mac, Knox had said. He made the world in seven days. That's what I call bluidy diligent.

Okay. But how could we have a thrifty God when by definition God is not interested in currency?

Hard cash, Knox had said. He's interested in cash flow analysis, laddie. It's as easy for God to be a Scotsman as it is for Charlie Tully to play for Ireland. What do ye say that we adjourn to a little hostelry on the High Street and belt a few back?

Certainly, Knox had entertained a few curious notions at that time. He remembered how, after downing a few Red Hackles, Knox had recited several verses of McGonagall and had followed as an encore with a dramatic rendition of Columba reaching Iona and entering into secretive land negotiations with the factor.

He closed his eyes, his lips fixed around the rim of his cup. He saw the woman in the mouth of the cave: she would interfere with history, with his spider. One finger cocked, she was making an unmistakable gesture, inviting him to step outside for a lewd purpose. He imagined a vulgar dance that would lead him all the way down to Ballantrae, where he had no desire to go. He suddenly saw reams of Scotsmen leaping over the Canadian edge. He imagined them kilted in sub-tropical jungles, smoking hemp with native persons; he saw them lingering outside bars in Sydney, waiting for the doors to open; saw them idly spinning coins in dark American cities; saw them building highways across New Zealand; hacking down huge rubber plants in Burmese jungles; teaching the pacifist sport of football to a group of sloe-eyed chicanos in some Mexican resort; discussing McTaggart's concept of

Time in civilized lounges in Canadian colleges; reciting the complete works of Barbour to groups of yawning Germans in Edinburgh motels; shipyard workers debating the pros and the cons of nightlife in Largs as they walked down the Govan Road . . . His was a race of explorers and inventors, responsible for tarmacadamizing half of the world and for inoculating the other half against various bacteria. Proud, and rightly so, he thought; and holding out still against the menace that crept, like some primeval protoplasmic gell, up and around the environs of Berwick-on-Tweed.

Last week, had he not read in the *Sunday Post* of how an intrepid adventurer from Wemyss Bay had travelled all the way from John O'Groats to Wigan in a wheelbarrow? Was that not the spirit? the stuff?

Through his mind, in a demented manner, there now echoed a mélange of old songs. A young girl seemed to be saying to him: I am a Dundee Weaver, come step inside this close with me and I will show you a thing or two; a huge yawning mouth was espousing the cause of Glasgow Rangers, singing Follow Follow; another preferred the jingo, Tiger Shaw never saw where Charlie Tully put the baw. He sat enthralled by the melodic debris of his broken-down cerebral structures. He sat looking at a piece of mouldy bread, thinking of penicillin.

Professor Saltash, meanwhile, was scrutinizing the Lecturer's wife, whose pale and suffering face had surfaced around his office door a short while ago; and now she sat, a handkerchief in her fingers as though she were holding a flag at half mast, a tear in the eye, a quiver around the lower lip. The Professor was not at ease with human suffering for he thought it implied a certain philosophical disregard for the innate concept of the general flux of reality: this subtle idea, granted, could simply be reduced to a manageable platitude as in: Look on the bright side of things; or Tomorrow will be much better, wait

83

and see. The Professor, however, would not shame himself by uttering these phrases. He had dipped into the work of Alfred North Whitehead in his time: and, as a hobby, he often read McTaggart, whose work he had often thought of popularizing in tiny pamphlets to be distributed amongst shipyard workers and students.

The woman said: 'I am, not to put too fine a point on it, I am at my wits' end.'

Professor Saltash, who thought he had a way with women, given his crooked smile, now demonstrated that smile as a matter of sympathy: 'Dear lady,' he said. 'Remember what Heraclitus said. Don't be fooled by clocks.'

'Clocks?' asked the woman.

Thinking that he was being perhaps too obtuse, Saltash added: 'Time is not a meaningful thing.'

'But I am at my wits' end,' the lady said, adjusting her hat. 'He does not know me. Yesterday I found him writing a letter to Flora McDonald at a *poste restante* address in Skye ... Just imagine.'

'It bears out my point, dear lady,' said the Professor, who had found himself thinking incongruously of how the Kelvin nuzzled its way into the Clyde and of how the Clyde flowed outwards towards the Atlantic. 'It underlines the very thing I am trying to tell you about ... namely, time. Clocks. Time-pieces. Grandfather clocks. Little Swiss miniatures. Mickey Mouse watches. Chronometers. Don't you see? It all means nothing.'

The lady looked at him for a while, wondering why she had come to this place for advice and counsel, why she had walked into his office as though it were a confessional of a kind. Dismayed somewhat, she looked out of the window.

'What's that noise?' she asked. 'Is that the Kelvin?'

He put a record upon the turntable of his old gramophone: it was of the First Battalion The Queen's Own Cameron

Highlanders playing *The 79th Farewell to Gibraltar*. He listened, eyes closed, to the melancholic music in whose succulent phrases he could envision the silver leap of a salmon in freezing water; the upward-reaching grandeur of a Douglas fir; Princes Street, Edinburgh, viewed as if from a helicopter's cabin; a relaxed long-shot of the city of Perth where it lingered above the Tay; a steaming plate of Forfar Bridie and mashed potato: his mind had become, briefly, a calendar of the pictorial kind that anxious mothers send to their exiled sons in faraway places. The Scotland of some technicolour dream, a vast rustic sprawl of majestic mountains, charming granite cottages, picturesque high streets in such villages as Auchtermuchtie, a parochial wedding in the one and only street of Auchmithie, Angus, dangling dangerously upon the lip of a cliff, old ruined castles and keeps smoothed blue by artificial moonlight, such as the broken tower at Lochranza on the Isle of Arran, it was a Scotia of the mind, a geography of the brain, the inspiration of some hallucinated cartographer whose lenient eye overlooked such trifling matters as slums, unemployment, immigration and the high incidence of alcoholism. It was his Scotland, impregnable, uncontaminated by the rodent English, the Scotland whose name was triumphantly cried, in a hyphenated form, in the stadium of Wembley; wept over at New Year's Eve in Saskatchewan, Alberta, Nova Scotia and Rio de Janeiro; whose sound was whimpered and whispered as though it were an arcane pronunciation of that which has no name; the Scotland that had entrusted the planet with *Auld Lang Syne* and had been generous with its tiny souvenir bagpipes; whose tartans were sported by the French in such places as Marseilles; the country that Americans dreamed in their most secret dreams, the country they longed to find their heritage in and subsequently paid good dollars to genealogical horticulturists who could whip up a phoney family tree before you could say the secret name of Jack House; whose mists were trapped and canned and exported to smogbound Californians who did not dream that the world could smell so good; whose whisky was broken down and analysed and fruitlessly counterfeited by cunning Japanese in places called Dun-Mac-Dee or Fort Willi-Am or Glen Urk-Art; whose grey towns were sent abroad on a million picture-postcards; whose people went forth into virgin and often hostile territories for the purpose of conquering restless natives; whose accents gave the name of the Christ an extra r, and therefore an unexpected ruggedness; this was his Scot-land, his own, his very own, Scotland.

The record stopped. The troops left Gibraltar, heading for Flodden Field and wonderful disaster. He opened his eyes, thinking of Glasgow all around him, the city that burned like some gross monster trapped upon the presbyterian night. And his heart, no longer a cartilage, a mere pump, became the embodiment of some crude spirit. He thought of a quarter of a million people sending James Maxton off from Central Station to do business with the devils of Westminster. He thought of gunboats hanging lobsterlike at the mouth of the Clyde. He thought of mutton pies, the Broons on Sunday, of A. J. Cronin, of the troops ensconced in the Maryhill Barracks and awaiting the call to mutiny. He thought of Pakistani bus-conductors with broad regional accents. He thought of going out and peering into the heart of the city. And he rose, dropping the tartan rug all about him; and out he went in the fashion of an explorer whose pursuit is the innermost citadel of English subterfuge.

As he left the yard, a small band played *The Bonnie Lass of Fyvie* and he marched up Byres Road, saluting people willy-nilly in a military fashion. Observing him from the shell of a Panda patrol-car, PCs Williams and McHardy decided, after some argument and a call to Headquarters, that he was harmless and should be allowed to proceed. As he proceeded, he noticed how sad and sullen his people looked, almost as if they had allowed memories of their heritage to disintegrate; no doubt this was in part due to the airwaves being stuffed with TV pictures of the British Empire and how Victoria had been its Great Architect and Sir Kenneth Clark, or someone who looked like him, its Supreme Apologist. Faggots! Maggots! He would have none of that stuff!

He walked in the direction of the University now, where good students filled their days planning monstrous Rag Week schemes. And fornicated in bushes. And in closes. And held wild parties. And smoked marijuana. And terrorized the local populace with words of three and sometimes even four syllables. He entered the University grounds, possessed of the notion that whatever was now troubling him could be resolved in the course of a confrontation with Professor Saltash. He was suspicious of Saltash as indeed he suspected all dreadful pseudo-Scots, Scots of the absentee-landlord variety, those who persisted in double-barrelling their names as if in the faint hope that at least one part of the hybrid would indicate good blood and a fine heritage: as in Maxwell-Levy, Duncan-Schwartz, Campbell-Itsibushi. Saltash, he knew, had been born in the English city of Rugby, educated there at the public school, and later – unfortunately – at the resort town of St Andrews where he had diligently acquired a burr that fooled the English but nobody else.

The band played on: *The Bonnie Lass of Fyvie.*

Waiting the return of her husband, the Lecturer's wife recovered from her earlier alarm at finding him absent, and began to read a story – her feet up on a beaten leather pouffe that had become shapeless over the years – in the latest edition of *The Red Star Weekly*, a magazine devoted to the coy exchange of affections between country doctors and thin librarians, a world in which there were neither sins of omission nor those of inclusion: 'a gentle kiss on closed lips' meant that what was taking place was a gentle kiss on closed lips. It was all terribly subtle, but she had the knack of reading between the lines.

Now she read:

'Alex had misunderstood Fiona's remark about Jill and her fiancé Ralph, which concerned the reception at the manse and something that had been whispered between Robin and Meggan. Alex was determined to make amends because something in his heart had been touched by Fiona, by her thin appearance, her pretty mouth, and the way she did her hair. I hope it's not too late, Alex thought . . .'

Palpitations. Heartbeats. Clammy palms. Nerves. She turned the page:

'The manse stood on the edge of the cliff. Beneath it he could hear the anger of the tide. Then he saw, outlined against the grey sky, the slim shape of someone. Was it Fiona? Or had Meggan returned? Could it be Flora? Or was it Davina, the last person in the world he expected to see? No, he thought: it has to be Frances.'

He looked at Saltash across the spacious office wherein hung several academic diplomas and old photographs: one of which, in a blurry sense, depicted Saltash disguised as a rugby player.

'How are you feeling?' the Professor, a little alarmed, asked.

'Just give me the facts,' said the Lecturer. 'How do you plan to deploy your men at Flodden?'

'I think that's my business,' Saltash answered, perhaps too quickly.

'Ah! Then you admit you're an Englishman?' The Lecturer, somewhat crazed, leaped upon the desk and brought his fist down as if this feeble weapon, albeit attached to an equally feeble arm, were the very Hammer of the English.

'I'm proud of it, sir,' said Saltash. 'But shouldn't you be napping right now?'

'Napping? I protest that suggestion! You ask me to sleep while your ruffians are sneaking through the heather?'

'Well, not quite,' said Saltash. 'You ought to relax a little before the . . . coming fray.'

The Lecturer stood upright by the window, a firm silhouette: he could hear the Kelvin muttering down towards the Clyde.

'I warn you, Saltash. I'll despatch your men without ado!'

Sweeping the tartan rug around his shoulder, a rug he had in fact left behind, the Lecturer disappeared from the office.

The woman was saying to him: 'Our candidate, Mr Bute, actually changed his name by deedpoll when we adopted him. In reality, he's called Martin Smith, but he changed the name to Alexander Fleming Graham Bell McKay Bute. It was a nice touch, was it not? The other candidates are both called Willie McNab, and neither has a distinguishing middle initial. Politics is wonderful and exciting.'

She observed that she was making no impression on her husband, who sat despairingly hunched beside the dying philodendron. She looked at herself in a mirror, thinking: I am growing old too fast. It is the strain. It is the strain most surely. She took a paper bag from beneath her chair and handed it to him.

'What's this?' he asked.

'A little present. It may cheer you.'

He saw the Sassenach wherever he looked. 'What's in the bag?' he asked.

'It will help you pass the time,' the woman said. 'It is a jigsaw puzzle.'

He stared at her hat which reminded him of a nightmare concerning bats and other furry flying mammals.

'A jigsaw puzzle?' he asked.

'It has three thousand interlocking pieces, an ambitious structure. When fully assembled it depicts the south view of

Melrose Abbey.' She smiled, hoping that he might in return smile; but he remained relentlessly dour. He had no time to spend over a puzzle that might take years to assemble, and besides, he had never thought of Melrose Abbey in an aesthetic way. It would altogether be a waste of valuable time.

The woman sighed: 'What do you think?'

He did not answer. There was a battle to be fought.

'Are you . . . I mean,' she said, sighing further; 'are you worried about your . . . troops, sir?'

'Worried? No, they're fine fighting men,' he replied.

He had looked inside one of the tents, noticing a young lady at work on a piece of paper. He had enquired into the nature of her literary labours, to learn that she was composing a poem to be called, perhaps, *The Flowers o' the Forest*, a sad epic concerning tomorrow's battle. She read him a few verses, which he found too melancholic for his own taste, but which nevertheless he could appreciate in the abstract. Keep up the good work, he had told her. He made his round of the tents encouraging his captains and his lieutenants, talking of gory beds and Scots Wha Hae and other related ethnic matters. A young sergeant stepped from a tent and said, in an optimistic way: 'Clanjamfrie. Flibbertigibbet. Whatjamacallit.'

He had saluted this soldier, admired his courage, longed for strength, prayed aloud to God on the field overlooking Flodden. In other tents, almost as if they were unaware of the ensuing conflict, several enlisted men played Monopoly and argued over property rights. Chalked on a rough stone wall was the slogan: *Sean Connery for Pope*. He admired the simplicity of this. Tonight, in fact, there was not much that he did not admire. He admired all manner of things. He admired the songs of his soldiers and the way they played Monopoly. He admired the moonlight on his tent. He admired the young lady's poem. He admired her haunches. Tomorrow there would be war against the Sassenach pig. He admired that prospect, too.

The woman said: 'If I can help, sir, in the matter of nursing the wounded, do ask me.' And she sighed, somewhat piercingly.

He looked at her: 'You should be in your tent, woman.'

'But a woman can have a place in battle, sir.'

'I'll not disagree with that,' he said, wondering who this stranger with the haunted expression and sagging titties might in reality be: but in war, you know, people came and they went, and it was no time for firm relationships.

He saw lamps burning all down the lines of the encampment. He heard Scottish soldiers singing *Follow, Follow, If You Go To Flodden We Will Follow On*. He admired the simple courage of this song. The air was warm, heathery, the late and dying sky filled with curving swallows. He wondered what might have happened to Eric Caldow had not this audacious full-back broken his leg. He knew the full depth of hatred, an abrupt sensation, something he had not entirely expected. He heard a slight wind flapping around the tents. In the morning, when the air was thick with English arrows, and when one particular historic arrow would be pinned to his gullet, he would still hear the echo of his soldiers' singing and remember lines of the young woman's poem, which he admired.

The woman said to him: 'Sir, why not pass your time before the battle by doing this jigsaw puzzle of Melrose Abbey?'

He stared at the cardboard box, the falsified colours, the south view of the cumbersome structure. He looked briefly at the woman, who was in the act of rising from her chair.

'I'll bring some hot cocoa, if you would like that,' she said.

'Hot cocoa,' said the man, as though he were echoing some half-forgotten phrase that now returned, in the manner of an unexorcized spook, to haunt him with dragging chains.

'Yes, hot cocoa.'

The woman stepped into the kitchen and out of the front lines of the battle. She placed a brass kettle upon the gas-stove, struck a match, listened to the muffled whisper of the flame igniting. She looked at herself in a mirror that hung askew above the sink. It is the strain, she thought. The worst thing is the strain. And she sighed, for sighing had become the protest and the retreat of her life, and, carrying two cups of rather too hot cocoa, she stepped back out into the conservatory to the lines of warfare, the passageways of history, the corridors of some odd madness, disturbing – even if she did not know it – the flight of an arrow that, whinging out of some taut English crossbow, was coming straight and true for the good King's vulnerable gullet and that would release, in all its broken majesty, the flow of a Scotsman's blood.

THE MOTHER-LODE

Arthur Young

To say that we were poor would be wrong: but there was in our lives a constant calling to canniness, a daily devotion to making do, a perpetual coping with paucity.

Not that our home was unusual.

In every airt of that coal-town, generations had been bred to being spare.

Grandparents, uncles and aunts, family friends, my running mates in every pend and close: all were thirled to thrift. Second hand and skimping, almost enough and nearly new: these, the iron rations of dearth were our daily dree.

The endless champing on this hard tack seemed to serve a double purpose.

In some way it placated the orthodox Presbyterian God, who frightened me in Sunday school. But more important, it was a sacrifice to those pagan ikons seen from all corners: the colliery winding wheels. At all costs they must be kept whirring in their stark, latticed towers.

The awfulness of their wrath, the great wreaking of poverty that came when they were stopped, affected the whole community with a primal fear. We were no exception.

Indeed, the matter was raised to the passion of a religion by my mother: and the bethel of her bawbees was a twist-clasp purse, snapped shut and sacrosanct. For further reverence, it was kept in the depths of her big, brown bag, bathed in a rich incense of mint imperials and lavender.

I must make it clear, though, that this was not because she had a mean nature: nor was she of a miserly disposition.

It was because of my father.

Although he was not a miner; although he was saved the vicissitudes of that master-ridden trade, he had a flaw which made his situation even worse.

Where money was concerned, he was a fool.

It left his fingers. It fell through his pockets. It just disappeared.

It was not that he was unduly reckless, or that he gambled or drank to excess, as many of the harsh men did. I think in some ways my mother could have borne that more easily.

No, it was just that he was feckless as flotsam, in contrast to my mother, who held fast in those chill currents with a kedge of common sense.

He was an easy touch: a soft mark for a hard luck story: openhanded in a loose, careless way that was an affront to my mother's frugality:

'Ye never lent money to him! Oh, Alec! He'll juist drink it! And what about me, Alec? What about me? It's not fair! It's not! Oh, *when* will ye get it back?'

And her tears ran in rage and vexation.

He would cajole:

'Och! Mirrin! Yuill get it back next week! Promise! Sure as death!'

Death came often in those days: in the fever van or at the hot, wet coal face. But the promises did not.

He loved to spend. He would shell out as long as there was money in his pocket.

He was a great man for a pound:

'Here's a pound!' he would say.

You could tell he liked the sound of himself saying it.

But once it was broken, he would not rest content until it was all gone.

He was compelled to stupid extravagances: to useless squandering.

Not that he was selfish:

'See! Mirrin! Here's some Toblerone!' hoping to bribe

away her scolding.

'Alec! You shouldn't! Ye know ye shouldn't!'

We would all have some of the honeyed, chocolate triangles: but you could see she didn't enjoy it.

She waited for the guilt, the admission, that always came: and which was never sweet.

At these times she had a habit of holding her bag in her arms with a firm hand on the clasp.

She could not trust him to pay a bill. He would come back and his slack smile told its own story, before he spoke. He had found some other road for the money.

Friday nights were a misery for my mother until she got his pay packet safe. If he met a chancer, or was attracted by some bright shop window, her reckoning for the week would be ruined. Sometimes it was many weeks.

In his easy come and go ways during those stern years, he was the exception that threatened our security: and so made my mother's rules the stronger.

In time I came to recognize the terrible truths with which she grappled: and to understand the worth of her rock-fast stability, around which the poorness of our society forever lapped and lipped.

But this understanding did not come to me early.

He was especially soft with me: and this insidious blackmail paid off for years.

He was forever slipping me lucky bags or sugarally pipes: 'Don't let on!'

I guzzled the illicit liquorice all right: but even then I sensed that something was wrong.

At nights I would go to the shop where he worked and wait outside for him to finish. In his white apron and coat, in the bright winter lights, busy with customers, and pulling the lever to make the little brass cash cylinders crash and clash along the overhead wires to the counting house, he seemed brisk, assured, confident.

But on the way home he could be pulled this way and that. I wheedled his favour. I sidled with him for treats. I made up to him for extras.

My mother found out though: always.

She railed:

'Yuill have him fair spoiled before yuir finished!'

'Ach! He's only a wean. Let him be!'

My mother gave me my regular, meagre pocket money. I had to work for that: errands, chores.

'That's all yuir getting from me!' she would say and snap shut the clasp on her purse.

In our glance at these times was a full understanding of my duplicity: but she never said more.

In time there was a funny effect: I became ashamed to show her affection. To hug or kiss her seemed a sort of dishonour. I could not cheat her twice.

So my mother fought with her enemy: alone.

She used left overs again and yet again:

'Yuill can have that het up tomorrow for yuir tea!' or 'There'll be enough if I put in some doughballs.'

But we were never hungry like some I knew.

She darned socks: then darned the darns. But I was never barefoot like some of the children in the low-town rows.

She patched shirts and made new collars from the tails. But my father had a bene suit, and I had blue serge shorts and a grey woollen jersey without holes, for the Kirk.

On Sunday nights, though, he couldn't spend. The Lord put up the shutters and he had nowhere to go for a buying breenge.

He would lift things to do and lay them down unfinished.

Often we had on our fret-faced wireless: but even that palled.

He would pull a chair across and fiddle with the tuning knob.

Mostly he got eerie atmospherics: but sometimes when the

needle passed Athlone or Daventry or Brno there was music
or talk:

'Listen! Listen! All that way! We'll go there some day. So
we will. Wait and see!'

The grunts and howls made me shiver. They must come
from the very depths of the universe I thought. These places
must be in other ethereal worlds where the dimensions would
be strange and the landscapes scaring.

I would huddle my three-legged stool close to the range
and look at my mother.

She would nod at me to show the world was in her control
and knit away on four steel pins.

His talk excited me: no doubt.

But I drew comfort from the warm fire, the curtained bed,
and the quiet skiddling of the jaw box tap.

Most of all though, I felt the presence of the big, brown
bag snuggled in at her back. Didn't it hold all the love that
ever was?

Two special events happened every year.

Such luck was not common. That they ever came at all was
wholly due to my mother and the skilly way she salted away
spare silver.

But on the day she gave my father his place. The purse was
emptied and the coins changed to pound notes for him to stuff
in his pockets.

It was for him to disburse the money.

Mind, before he appeared to the world as a spending man,
she always had a go at him:

'Now! Yuill be careful, Alec!'

'Aye, wumman! Aye!' he would agree with grievance in his
voice. Was he not to be trusted?

After that she said little; kept her hard sayings in check.
But you could see that it was often an effort.

One event was a holiday in the summer time. We went to a

boarding house by the seaside.

I paddled among the white pebbles, washed and lustrous, and with no coal smirr to spoil them. Afterwards there were chocolate eggs from a cast-iron hen, and sliders with red, sweet stuff.

'He'll be sick, Alec!'

'No' him, he'll no'!' said my sponsor.

I stuffed myself before the money would go done, or before my mother's thinned lips would give way to a row and blanket repression of all soft options:

'Come and we'll have some, Mirrin!' he would cajole at the teashops:

'No! I'll wait for my right tea!'

'I'll buy you one of these!' he would urge, jovial and flush with cash. And it might be a hat or a trinket for her person.

Perhaps only I suspected her inner longing to accept: but she never did.

I do remember, though, that in those boarding houses there was always a bath and there was hot water if you asked. She loved this and would ask several times in the week.

She also liked sitting behind the big silver teapot and getting the serving girl to bring hot water.

On the way home my father would urge:

'That was great, eh? We'll go for longer next year! We'll go farther away! Maybe to England!'

I noticed that when he made wild remarks like that, my mother rattled her fingers on the big brown bag, now empty; waiting to be filled again in careful dribs and drabs.

'Maybe! We'll see!'

But she lacked his enthusiasm.

The second event happened in winter, around Christmas.

We had a whole day in the town: a pantomime, then high tea in a shop, and a visit to the Kelvin Hall.

We went to the Princess Theatre matinee. We sat on the steep wooden seats of the gallery. It was always George West and a funny title:

'It's got thirteen letters!' explained my father. 'It's the same every year. Count them!'

TAMMY TOODLEUM I counted: he was right.

Again he was in his element, spending, spending.

'Alec, ye mustn't!' my mother would insist.

But he waved away her worries.

One year it all went wrong, never to come right.

It started in the theatre: at the interval.

I had an ice-cream from a cardboard carton. My mother would have settled for the same.

But my father got his eye on some ladies being served with tea and dainty biscuits on little trays. They were in the circle below us:

'Here, miss! We'll have some tea on a tray like that!'

The reply was simple: yet it stunned all other senses and left shame as the only sensation.

'That's not for up here! Only the circle and the stalls!'

The ridicule washed around and over us in snorts and not so quiet remarks. You must never, ever get above yourself in Glasgow.

My mother snatched her bag to her breast in instinct: but the darts were home. Red poison stained her neck to cock's comb hue. Black affront silted up the leaders in her neck, making them stand out.

After one terrible look at my father, she stared away from him and at the stage: but she only saw some sad performance.

Although my father and I were carried away by the hilarious antics on the stage, enough to forget and to laugh, her face stayed stark and sombre.

Usually we had tea in a Ross's dairy. Once we had even gone to the Poly where there was a little band.

That day my mother said:

'I want to go home.'

Her face was a funny colour: pale with a grey tinge.

I was startled and in fear. Was I to lose my treat?

'Ach, Mirrin! Ye can't do that! What about him, the wean! He'll be disappointed!'

She shook her head in tiny movements, as if to shake off a fly.

'All right! All right!'

But her voice was a whisper and barely heard in the busy theatre corridor.

There was no holding my father then. He would show them, us, everyone. He would be the grand man and count no cost: I could tell. A bit of a splash and the last upset would be soon forgotten.

He insisted on a posh place.

Even I hung back, uneasy at the snow-white cloths, the starch-dusted waiters.

My mother hissed:

'Alec! Alec!'

But my father ignored everything and marched past the crowded tables, to one empty and by a window.

'Alec! Alec! Is this all right?'

Her whole face was tinged pink now.

'Aye, wumman! Aye! We'll be fine here!'

He insisted that we take off our outdoor things – there were so many buttons and belts among us – and sit down.

A severe man in a tail suit came up. I was surprised to see that his penguin plumage, so black and elegant from a distance, was in fact shiny with use, and slittered and stained.

'We'll have high tea!' ordered my father.

He meant to be decisive, a man to give orders, with money at his back. Instead his tone was brittle and sharp.

The reply shattered any self-esteem, cracking it like a nutshell, and leaving the raw kernel of spirit exquisitely tender:

'We don't serve high teas! Dinner only!'

My father tried to save the day:

'We'll have the dinner then!'

'This table is reserved!'

He made a last attempt:

'Another table – !'

'Not a table in the place – sir!'

The last word dropped in place after a long, long second. We had been dismissed with gravy and soup-spattered disdain. We were not his sort.

Hunger healed my own humiliation on the spot. I wanted a tea shop with tomato-sauce on the table and baking smells to make the juices run.

But a glance at my mother showed that this was in doubt.

She rose and swept up her coat and gloves. She cuddled her precious, precious bag as if to squeeze out some talisman protection.

My father was silenced by her face. It showed great strings and ridges of strain: and the limit of her endurance was clear about her eyes, which were cradled in a fine mesh of crinkled and crazed skin folds.

As she fastened herself into her outdoor things again, I could see that she was doing it by feel and touch. Her vision was entirely inward: and it was utterly bleak.

We had tea in time, in modest surrounds. I felt more at home. My mother ate nothing, but asked the waitress if she could have some aspirin tablets. She swallowed two and drank many cups of tea.

At the end of the meal once more she said:

'I want to go home! Now!'

Once again my father pleaded: wheedled.

'Mirrin! The wean likes the shows. He'll be upset!'

She shook her head at him: but it was in some kind of disbelief.

He knew as well as I, but he chose to misread her silence:

'We'll just go for an hour, eh?'

For that hour he outdid himself.

I realized that I was an excuse: but I wantonly joined in his folly.

I wanted to turn to her, to show her I knew: but then I might lose my chance of spoil.

'C'mon! We'll go on this!'

We went round and round.

'Want to try this!'

We were shaken up and down.

We went on everything that moved. We threw balls and rings and darts.

My mother was loaded with glass dishes, and celluloid dolls with feather skirts. Of course, we had to have a coconut, although it took my father umpteen tries.

He spent threepences and sixpences until we were dizzy and tired, deafened with noise and dazzled by the lights that flashed on and off.

He asked my mother time and again to join us: but she said no.

I had never seen her look or act like that before. She had a dazed, uncertain manner. Sometimes she did not seem to hear. Once or twice my father took her by the arm and steered her among the side shows, as if she was lost.

In her arms and hands she clutched the gew-gaws which had cost so dear. Half-hidden among them was her bag. It seemed incongruous and curiously small.

When the money in his pocket was finished, we set out for home. He had had his day until next time.

But, although I did not know it then, although it took some time to dawn, I had had my day for ever.

Through the years I have grown a reputation for penny pinching. I acknowledge it freely. I hope I am not ungenerous: but I will walk a mile to save a coin.

I hoard things. Although they can have no possible use I save rusted screwnails, odd lengths of wood, old electrical fitments with the copper green and greasy.

My son, the accountant one, flights at me:

'What d'you want all this money for? Take Mother for a trip round the world! Or buy a house in Spain and spend the winter there!'

But I've only ever seen pictures of the Taj-Mahal; and my wife, good soul, watches the rain with me.

NOCTURNE/two

Carl MacDougall

The street wasn't crowded. Walking home alone in the first light of an early early morning with a few clouds still between me and the stars. The moon was over the university. It outlined the galleries and threw gold across the park where a few couples were finishing up and going home. An old man was sleeping on a bench, his head resting on a parcel of newspapers.

I thought of mid-afternoon and nothing to recall the now of it, the peace, the joy and the beauty of the morning, walking home. And there was nothing to recall my mother, small as a lion in her good coat, clutching her handbag, changing her voice for our Sunday outing, my hand tight and warm in hers: Miss Beveridge says you're clever enough to have your name up on these gates.

Father's hopes were that I leave school able to write my name and count my pay. Father died and Mother lived. In a sense, I am very fortunate. I fulfilled the ambitions both parents had for me. Mother wanted me to go to university, because I don't want you to go the way your father went, she said.

I went, hated it, but grew to love the nineteenth-century parthenon where God stayed; its open doors, its six columns, its passivity and its peace. I never went to a service: damn the fear of it. I went to be alone. Once I went for advice. The minister was in a hurry, but awarded me some of his time: I think it would be ludicrous for you to leave, whatever the reason. Society needs young men; graduates, trained and educated. No, I think you should stick at it; get your head down, wire in. You have a good head on your shoulders and you are privileged insofar as you are being given an opportunity to use it. Society is full of frustrated young people who don't know which way to turn because they have never had the opportunity to realize their potential, and here you are, ungratefully wanting to throw it away. Prayer. That's the answer. Prayer. Pray for the power to accept and to realize your potential. Get rid of that other silly business and get on with your studies. But don't forget: prayer.

I didn't know what the word meant. Remaining silent and still while someone else was talking, a dark dream of the Jesus face coming smiling forward, church four times on a Sunday, my grandfather's black suit and Come-to-Jesus collar, no *Sunday Post*, the woman with the issue of blood and I the Lord thy God am a jealous God visiting the iniquity of the fathers upon the children, singing *Guide Me Oh Thou Great Jehovah* till my insides trembled. I didn't know any more.

Father's women made Mother very unhappy, so she made a promise I had to keep. I shuffled around, sniffing for reality, peeling into the onion layers like an inexperienced exotic dancer. The stronger the scent, the less I liked it. I listened to my head and the bad thoughts made me feel guilty.

Make me a circus, she said, and me lying there wondering what she meant.

I could live with neither one, the other, nor both. I didn't know any nice girls and didn't want to spend Sundays taking Mother for a run in the car. I wanted to lie with her chattering about clothes, listening to Indian music that hung around the room like a scent. But she never managed to make me comfortable. I always left and walked home through the park. And Mother always waited up for me.

Why don't you stay? she asked. It's funny, I can't tell you, can't put it into words, but I hate it when you go. I lie for hours, wondering if you've got home all right; remembering. Sometimes I think of things I'll do or make for you. But

I can't make anything, nice, so as you'd like it. Then I want you to make things for me. I think of what we'll do together, what I'll say, but I never remember any of it when you're here. Why don't you come more often? And why don't you stay? No, I'm all right. Just hold me close. Let me feel you next to me. And she rocked me slowly.

Sometimes I think my body is fed up having me as tenant. The food is lousy and the hours are long. But on this mother of pearl morning I was alive and well and felt better than God. There was a lovely morning smell, across the grass, up the hill, towards the rhododendron clump. I watched the stealthy way the policeman came into the park, muted his radio, looked around him, fumbled with his fly buttons and leaned back with a sigh as his arc sprayed the rhododendrons. As I passed and said, Good morning, I swear to God the bare-faced bastard blushed.

But that was a bonus. I was decided and for once I felt beloved.

KEEN

Peter Chaloner

It was a couple of weeks after the New Year. Me and my
mother. You should have seen the row we had. She's going to
marry this new man. And me and my big brother were fighting all the time. Couldn't seem to get on. So she told me to
get out. She didn't want this new man getting the wrong impression. Didn't want him thinking she'd brought up a
couple of neds. That's what she said. But she just wanted rid
of me.

I swore at her. There was just me and her in the house. The
dishes were flying. But I was glad to be getting away, really.
Away from her. And Corby. And that daft job in the steelworks.

'Mother.' That will be right. She never looked after me and
my wee brother properly. She's not got the brains for it.
That's the truth. She's thick. Not bad looking. Specially on
a Friday night when she gets dolled up. But she's thick.
That's how me and James got brought up in the Children's
Home.

Anyway. This night of the argument. I decided I was going
back up to Scotland. I kicked in her big mirror and a couple
of the ornaments I knew she liked. Then I walked out and got
the long distance bus up here. I got the money out her handbag. She was that scared she just handed it to me. Shaking
like a leaf. I'd turned sixteen just before Christmas. There
wasn't a thing anybody could do about it.

Not that a few quid'll last me very long. By the time I got
off the bus I was skint. So I went down to the Salvation
Army. One of the boys told me what you need to say to get

in with them. Orphan, looking for a job, all this carry-on. So
I said that and they got me digs with this old woman. She
put me out about three o'clock the third day. Pouring rain
and all. For coming in late to meals, supposed to be. So that
was me back up to see my Salvation Army Counsellor.

Everybody they take on gets a Counsellor. He's just an
ordinary bloke. Just somebody to tell you what to do next.
He says to me, 'I've got some pals starting up a maroonimus.'
He'd a very quiet voice. You could hardly tell what he was
saying to you. 'A what?' I says. 'A Community House,' he
says. 'I've got some pals starting up a Community House.
It's been going about five months. It doesn't look like you're
going to be happy in our usual sort of digs. Want to give it a
try?' I didn't know what kind of a House he was talking about
at all. But I was skint and soaking wet so I says okay. He gave
me my bus fare. That was the back of four o'clock.

It must have been near enough five by the time I got out
to the House. It was miles away. Right the other side of the
city. Out in these bits you never see. Wide streets full of
trees, and big houses that rich blokes built years ago. They
had a sign up in the garden. Big green board with shoogly
orange writing. It said IF YOU DON'T KNOW COME
AND LEARN. IF YOU DO KNOW COME AND
TEACH. I just went in anyway.

But I didn't fancy it. I like narrow streets. Modern houses.
Small rooms. Fitted carpets. New furniture. Colour telly.
The gas fire on all winter. And a stereo with all the charts
records.

That's what my mother's new man's got, down in Corby.
I get on well with him. He's a great runner. If him and me
are running for the bus, all you see is me belting along and
him flashing by me like a whippet. Table football. That's
another thing he's good at. They had a competition down at
the Corby club. Guess who won it. No bother. That's even
although it was five rounds and we'd a couple of pints in

between each round. Easy. We got a silver shield with our names on it. I'd a great time in his house. Watching the football and drinking cans of lager out the fridge. Fantastic.

This Community mob didn't have any of that. Standing about freezing in the dark. That's all they were good at. There was about twelve of them. All students. All years older than me. Doctors' lassies coming out to be doctors, and lawyers' sons coming out to be lawyers. A couple of school teachers. You want to have heard them talk. You wouldn't have believed it.

This dump they were in was about sixteen rooms. Hadn't been done up since it was built. That's going by the look of it. But listening to them you'd have thought it was something out of the Ideal Homes Exhibition.

It wasn't just a case of showing you round. They had to tell you what each room *was*. That's even although a blind man could have told you it was nothing. 'This is the Music Room.' There's egg boxes hammered all over one wall. So they think that makes it a Music Room. 'This is the Nursery.' One wean lived in the place. Belonged to one of the lassies that was a school teacher. It wasn't a year old yet. Couldn't even walk. But they had to have a room about forty feet square for it. 'This is the Joyful Silence Room.' That was the biggest laugh of the lot. A mucky old cupboard under the stairs. Stone floor. Slit window like a dungeon. If that's joyful the jail's hilarious. You'd have thought they were allergic to calling a room by its right name. 'Kitchen' wouldn't do them – they had to have a 'Cook Room' to go along with the 'Eat Room' next to it. The bathroom was the only place they couldn't think up a daft name for. There wasn't any hot water. They had cactuses growing in the bath.

The boss of the place was called 'Guy'. He was a big tough-looking bloke in a boiler suit. Nothing like me. He'd got a phone call from my Counsellor so he knew I was coming.

'I'll tell you straight,' he says to me. He said that a lot. The

voice he had – deep and English-sounding – you'd have
thought you were listening to the News at Ten. 'I'm in favour
of letting you move in here. I know you need a place, and
need is what this House is all about. But there won't be any
snap decision. We must make sure you'd be good for what
we're trying to achieve here. And we have to be sure the
House would help you grow.' In out the rain. That's all I was
wanting. But you couldn't tell him that. He claps me on the
back like a minister and walks away banging a frying pan with
a wooden spoon. He goes in and out all the rooms shouting:
'Council Meeting! Council Meeting after tea!' So while he's
occupied doing that, I go round breaking into all the old gas
and electric meters. Rubbish locks, they had on them. I got
seven quid in five-pence pieces. Planked them out the back.
You couldn't tell they'd been done, just looking at them. I
put back the locks just the way they were.

Guy saw me going up and down the stairs, in and out all
the rooms. He thought that meant I must be keen.

'I see you gave the place a good going-over,' he says to me.

'So I did,' I says. 'There's a lot of things here I'd like to
find out more about.'

Things I'd like to find out more about. I thought a lot about
that, before I said it to Guy. I'd heard him say it to somebody
else about two minutes after I got in the door. I decided that's
what he wanted to hear – just like the Salvation Army want
to hear you're an orphan looking for work. And I was right.
With him, you always had to be 'finding out more about'
something or other. You could never just stand, or just sit.
But then there's always something they want to hear you say.
In the Children's Home and the approved school it was the
same. If you want to get anywhere, you've got to find out
what these do-gooders want, and give it to them. Not just
near enough. Exactly. In their own words. If they call
black white, let them hear you calling it white. If they call
sitting about like a stookie doing nothing 'meditating',

remember that's what they call it. Then the next time they say 'What do you fancy doing now?' say 'Oh, I fancy doing a bit of meditating.' I'm telling you. It's the only way. It makes them think you're keen. Makes them think you don't laugh every time they turn their back.

That's the game I was up to at this Council Meeting. Not that any of them were fly enough to spot it. Giving them nothing only what they wanted to hear. Guy took me in to it. A Council Meeting was when the whole twelve of them sat down for a chat, instead of them all yattering amongst themselves as usual. They were all sitting round what they called the Eat Room, the whole twelve of them in a circle. Some of the women were sewing these old-fashioned clothes they wear. They seem to want to look like Tinks. One bloke about forty was sitting there putting the tail on a big red paper kite. I didn't know where to look. None of them was reading the paper. They never had a paper in that House. Or a telly. Too normal for them. They must've just had their tea. There was green and brown mush lying about on tin plates, and a pile of dirty chopsticks. I couldn't've eaten that stuff to save my life. Even though I was starving. When they asked me if I wanted any, I says no. So then the questioning starts. 'Where do you come from?' 'What makes you think you'd be good for this House?' 'Is there anything that means so much to you, you'd kill for it?' A lot of rubbish. But I knew how to speak to them. I just fed them back the words they fed me. Half the folk that asked me a question ended up making a speech anyway, so it was easy. By the time they decided I could stay – for a fortnight's 'Trial Period', supposed to be – I had them believing I'd been looking for a House like that for years.

Some of the blokes that didn't have to go in to college much had a van. They did odd jobs round about for money – 'Workforce', they called it. I told them I'd love to help out with that. I said I thought it was great, chipping in the most of what you earned. Just taking a few bob a week pocket money. I said I'd get up when the Workforce boys got up next morning – to 'find out more about' Workforce. Guy loved that. He went on Workforce every day. He told me at the end of the Meeting, if I got on well in the next couple of weeks, they'd need to think about electing me on to the Council.

Right after the Meeting, they all had Discovery Classes to go to. All except one skinny bloke with a two-foot-long beard – he had to wash all the dishes.

Discovery Classes was when folk that didn't live in the House were supposed to come up and 'find out more about' some daft thing or other. The old guy with the string ran what he called 'Kitemakers' Workshop'. The girl that had the baby ran 'Astrology Workshop'. A fat lassie with buck teeth ran 'Mime Workshop'. I says 'What is it?' She says 'Machines. Tonight we're all going to be factory machines.' Guy was down among the egg boxes with a pair of bongos. 'Drummers' Workshop.'

They had to call these things workshops seeing none of them ever did any work. Not real work. Not work like you do in the steelworks.

The laugh of it was too – outside folk wanted nothing to do with these Discovery Classes. Hardly anybody came up. And the two or three that did mostly took one look and went away again. You were lucky if you got three folk in one of these big dark cold rooms where a Discovery Class was supposed to be. Then Guy'd call a Meeting about it. 'We've not got enough variety.' 'We must advertise the Classes better.' They'd no idea. Folk didn't fancy their foosty old House. That was all about it. But you couldn't tell them that. They had to look for something complicated.

When Guy got his bongos out, I got off my mark. The rain was away. It wasn't even a cold night. I took my seven quid down the road and had a wee spree to myself.

First I got a box of chips and fried chicken from the

KEEN

American place I'd seen on the bus coming up. Hot food. Bright lights. The place packed. Charts records coming out of folks' trannies. You couldn't beat it. Then I bought a new shirt. It was a Thursday so the shops were open late. It was a cracker of a shirt. Pictures all over it. Shows you this toff in a dickey bow and a monocle and a top hat. I needed it. I'd nothing up with me from Corby. I put it on in a toilet in a pub. I just rammed the old shirt down the pan with the lavvy brush. It stank. Then I went through to the bar. Full belly. New shirt. Money in my pocket. I bought forty King Size and started sinking the pints of lager.

Don't ask me how many I had. It was a Disco bar. Music always makes me drink faster. Then about nine o'clock – I was well away by this time – they brought on this stripper. What a laugh. A fat old thing she was. Wobbly thighs. First thing she does she pulls off this old bloke's tie. Drags it between her legs. Then she shoves it under his nose. You should have seen his face. Then she comes round the whole company, getting different folk to undo the different bits of her outfit. I unhooked her cape. It fell on to the floor. Showed you the big chest she had on her. Like a pair of water wings. After that she goes back up to the old boy. He's still standing there holding his tie. She makes him bend down. Puts her left tit against his cheek. Then – wallop! – she belts her right tit good style and the old bloke's head goes BJOING! I just about pee'd myself.

Not long after that it was shutting time. Didn't seem long anyway. Then I was honking my load up against a cake shop window. I only had three five pences left. But I still had a full packet of Benson's.

I never got up the next morning. You can't. Not after a night like that. I got up about half three in the afternoon. Nobody in. The whole House empty. I went round all the rooms, but I couldn't see anybody and I couldn't find anything to eat either. Not what I would call food.

I found one good thing. A five pound note. Stuck in the jam jar in what they called 'The Shop'. It wasn't really a shop. It was just a big cupboard in the basement, stacked up to the ceiling with plastic bins full of rice and queer-looking stuff like rice but different colours – green and yellow and orange. Outside folk that knew about it could just walk in. Weigh themselves stuff – they had an old-fashioned pair of brass scales – and then walk out. Self service. They put the money in the jam jar. The prices were marked on the bins.

There was a good lot of change in the jar, along with the fiver, but I just left that. I didn't want anybody getting suspicious. So that was my finances fixed up again.

I went down the town and bought biscuits and went to see this Kung Fu picture. Great. I had a hot dog and a Coke and an ice cream in the interval. Then when I came out I bought a Kung Fu poster in the lobby. Brilliant poster. Shows you this wee guy getting strangled with this chain strung between two sticks. You see his tongue lolling out. Eyes popping out his head. Then I went across the road to the record shop and bought the new Number One. There was a record player back at the House. Nobody seemed to be using it. After that I bought a sausage supper and walked up the road eating it.

I kept more than half my sausage for Guy.

'Do you want this, Guy?' I says to him when I walked in. 'I can't finish it.' I could have finished it easy, but I wanted to keep in with him. He swallowed it in one bite. But he wasn't pleased.

'What happened to you this morning?' he says to me. 'Workforce. Remember? I spent fifteen minutes trying to wake you. I even tried picking you up, but you just fell back down again.' I couldn't very well say 'Sorry Guy, I was still drunk at the time.' So I just says 'Oh, I'm a very heavy sleeper. I'll get up after this. Honest. Want to hear my new record?'

By this time, I knew I had to play things their way for a

while. If I didn't want to get put out. And I didn't have a job or digs lined up yet. I hadn't even started looking. So for over a week I did everything they wanted. All except eat their food and go to their Discovery Classes.

They wanted me to sign on the Social Security. Put two-thirds of my dole money into House Funds. So I did. They wanted me to get out of my bed when it was still pitch black. Help Workforce build up some rich old dear's garden fence four feet higher so boys couldn't look in. So I did. They gave me this wee tiny room like a cupboard to sleep in. Told me to start thinking of it as my own. So I stuck up my Kung Fu poster. Talked about painting the walls red. Putting up shelves. All this carry-on. It kept them happy. Kept them thinking I was keen. In fact I did too good a job. They went and elected me on to the House Council. So then I had to go about for two days kidding on I was delighted about that.

But I was scunnered. That was the truth. I wanted away from the lot of them. I wanted among other folk that were sixteen. I wanted a normal job and my own place. Even just a job with enough cash for bevvy and a room somewhere would have done me. I checked the paper every night. But there was nothing doing. Or else: 'Wanted – Van Boy.' How am I supposed to live off the kind of wages a van boy gets? Once you take out the digs money, it's just a few quid. I need more than that for drink. Every night. That's not counting grub. It's not on. So that was me. I was short of a laugh.

That's how I got tied up with the motor scooter and Pat the Panhandler.

The scooter belonged to the old boy that did Kitemakers' Workshop. Every weekend he went runs on it, down to the shore and into the country. He was always saying to me, 'Come on along some Saturday, and we'll go hill climbing.' But I always says no. I didn't want to be seen hanging on the back like a big Jessie.

Then I started noticing the Kitemaker had a habit of

sleeping in front of the Eat Room fire after tea at night, if he didn't have a Class to go to. Half the time you could see the scooter keys sticking out his back pocket. So one night I just lifts them. Takes the scooter out for a ride. Up round all the schemes. Fantastic. You see all the other blokes that've got bikes looking at you. I'd a great time for about two hours. Then when I was parking the bike in front of the House again I got lifted. I wasn't wearing a helmet. Two police cruising by saw me and pulled me up.

First that was all it was. Riding without a helmet. But there was two cops and one of them was fat and keen. He starts asking me a lot of questions. Then it all comes out. No licence. No insurance. No L plates. The fat cop's getting madder every time he's got to write something in his book. 'Is it your bike at least?' he says to me. 'Naw,' I says. 'I live in there. The Community House. It's a bloke's in there. He gave me a shot of it.' 'Wait here,' he says. So me and the skinny cop are standing there. The fat one goes in the House. The door was always left open. He goes up the stair. Finds the Kitemaker still lying dozing in front of the fire. Kicks him. 'Have you got a motor scooter?' he says. The Kitemaker's that amazed, waking up and seeing the uniform, he says 'Oh no, don't tell me it's been stolen.' That made the fat cop really happy. He had me down to the Police Station and in a cell before I could say a word. Up on a charge. Theft of a Motor Vehicle.

'Very serious,' he says to me. He's closing that big iron door and laughing. 'You'll get time.'

As soon as they would let him, the Kitemaker came down and bailed me out. But that wasn't till the next morning, about ten o'clock. He took me in a café. 'Don't worry about a thing,' he kept saying to me. He wanted to buy me a big breakfast. But I wasn't taking charity. From him or anybody. 'The coffee alone'll do me fine,' I says. So then he starts telling me how everybody up at the House is right behind me. 'We all know you didn't mean to steal the scooter,' he says. 'And we'll get you properly defended. Don't worry about a thing. Some friends of mine are running a Legal Clinic. Meet me up at the University about one o'clock tomorrow and we'll get everything sorted out.' 'I'll be there,' I says. I left more than half the coffee in the cup.

Next morning I didn't feel like getting out of bed. You don't get a good sleep in a police cell. So I dogged the Workforce. Just lay in bed smoking fags till after two o'clock. When the Kitemaker came in that night he went off his head. Said he'd been standing waiting for me for twenty minutes. I wasn't caring. I didn't even tell him I was too busy to come. 'I was lying in my bed,' I says. 'I couldn't be bothered getting up.' He starts yelling at me. 'Who's doing who the favours?' he says. 'Think I care what happens to you?' And he walks out. Two seconds later he's back in. 'You don't *care* if you get put back inside,' he says. 'Being free. That means nothing to you, does it?' I just sits there blowing smoke rings. 'Not really,' I says.

I was glad to get the chance to annoy him. I didn't like what he was up to. He was covering up the real reason he was vexed. He hadn't got his chance to show me off to his pals up at the University. He'd missed his chance to show me off like a monkey. All this about me breaking my promise and that's how he was mad – that was just his lies.

Then I started to see that everybody in that House was telling me lies. 'The House will help you to grow' and all this. That was rubbish. They wanted me for a walking advert. That was their game. They had to be able to boast to folk – 'Our House tamed the wild man.' Everything else about the House wasn't working. Arguments every day amongst the folk that lived there. Nobody coming up to the Discovery Classes. The House was a flop. So they needed me.

See as soon as I got this worked out? I hated the lot of them from that time on. Up to now I'd felt like they were kids out the Special School. You can't hate kids out the Special School. There's nothing there to hate. But now? Now I knew I was going to let them in for it.

That's how Pat the Panhandler and me got to be pals. Him and me knew what this Community mob were worth. He got called 'The Panhandler' because, according to him, standing in the street asking folk you didn't know for ten pence was 'panhandling'. That was how he got all his cash. He was only about eighteen. But he didn't live anywhere and he never worked. One night when he was seventeen, he got fed up and set about his mother. They put him in the lunatic asylum. When he got out, he couldn't go back to his mother. So he just started sleeping the first place that was handy when he came out the pub at night. Sometimes he went up to the House and asked to sleep there. 'Crashing', he called it. He loved talking like a Yank. Sometimes Guy said okay, and charged him fifty pence. Other times he sneaked in the basement window and got to crash for nothing. Other times they turned him away.

This night, the Council finally decided they'd had enough of Pat. He wasn't to get to crash any more. They were fed up with how he was never around in the day and never did any work. Pat's just sitting there. Guy's screaming at him like a Zulu. 'I'll tell you straight, Pat!' he says. 'You're a parasite! If this was The Wild, I'd probably kill you!' Pat just shrugs. He couldn't have cared less. So they flung him out. I got him down the road. After that, I knocked about with Pat a good bit. It was the first time since Corby I'd had anybody to knock about with.

We were in the boozer every night. Spending whatever he'd managed to panhandle and whatever I'd managed to lift. You got a great laugh down there, with all the music and the fights. One night, a boy got flung right through the pub window. You should have seen his face. They'd a lot of good strippers too. Chinkies and darkies, all kinds. Whips, alligators – it was like a real show. In the day we'd maybe have a game of snooker. Or go round the big shops for a knock. Pat had a lot of good tricks for getting clothes for nothing. He needed a lot of new clothes. Most of the places he slept in were hoachy and you couldn't go down to the boozer dressed like a tramp. He was a right flash dresser. I copied all the styles off him.

Me and Pat were that busy, my Workforce caper went out the window. Guy was mad. The rest of the House gave me black looks. But it was water off a duck's back. To me, now, the House was just a place to sleep and a place to lift money. A couple of notes out a handbag or the shop jar every day. A handful of five pences out the electric meters every now and again. Apart from that, I wanted nothing to do with the place. Guy could lift me out of bed in the mornings. He did lift me out. That's how I kept waking up on the floor. But he couldn't make me go on the Workforce. Nobody could've. I wasn't kidding. That time of the day, I couldn't've stood up straight to save my life.

With the amount of cash I was lifting, folk in the House started to get sure it was me lifting it. But I wasn't worried. They could never prove a thing. I was too fly for them. Now and again I helped them look for money that was 'lost'. One night I handed in a fifty pence piece. Told them I'd found it under a heap of puppet clothes. They loved that.

All the same – one night the Kitemaker caught me with my hand in the shop jar. I don't know how he managed it. Even yet. I didn't go down to the shop till they were all at their tea. I counted the heads. But one minute I'm standing in the shop with my hand up to the wrist in the jar. Next minute the door opens. There's the Kitemaker right beside me. He doesn't say a word. He just slides the jar off my hand. Walks up the stair holding it. Up to call an Emergency Council Meeting. To get me put out.

I never believed they would do it. I thought if I got the

chance to look really sorry, the most of them would vote to let me get staying on. I wasn't worried. I stayed down in the basement another couple of minutes. Then I followed the Kitemaker up the stair.

Nobody says a word when I walk into the Eat Room. They're all sitting in a circle the way they were the first night. The shop jar's on the floor in the middle of the circle. Nobody even looks at me. Guy's the only one that comes up to me. He puts his hand on my back and guides me over to the shop jar. He hands me a cushion and says 'Sit here. I want to show you something.' Then he walks into the Cook Room. I just sits there letting my hair hide my face. Still nobody's saying a word.

Guy comes back. He's got a knife in his hand. It's got a bone handle and a blade about a foot and a half long. He puts it down at my feet and says in that deep voice like an advert, 'There are two ways. You must pick one. No more. Which is it to be? The way of the knife? Or . . . the other way?'

I felt a right dooley. Not for me. I was keeping a roof over my head. I knew what I was doing. For him. I got a red face, but it was for him. He must have thought he was on the telly. What's he expect me to do? Say the wrong answer? Say 'No, I want the way of the knife, chip me out on to the street' – ? I just does what anybody not daft would have done. I toes the knife. Skites it halfway across the room. I lets my head hang down and I says, quiet like, 'I'll take the other way.'

You should have seen Guy's face. You'd have thought he'd won the Pools. 'That's good enough for me,' he says. Then he claps my shoulder the way he did the first day and says, 'My vote is we let him stay.'

I thought that was me. I thought the rest of them would agree right away. They were in the habit of agreeing to whatever Guy wanted. But this time they weren't having it. Everything that had disappeared was my thieving. They were all sure of that. So they say I've got to get out.

Guy's that vexed at not getting his own way, he tells them they can put him out along with me. He starts screaming at them like he screamed at Pat. 'A boxful of dark is a boxful of nothing!' he says. 'Light can flow in! You don't believe that? Well I want nothing to do with you. Or your so-called Community.' And he tells the boy with the two-foot-long beard – the Treasurer – he wants his money back. Three hundred pounds. He inherited it in his grandfather's will and chipped it in, getting the House set up.

By this time they're all arguing amongst themselves. It's like a pub at shutting time. Everybody's shouting. All except the Treasurer. He's talking quietly. Trying to change Guy's mind for him. 'We don't have to settle this now,' he keeps saying. But Guy's too worked up. 'Oh yes we do,' he says. 'I've got to get out of here. It isn't just what happened tonight. There's no love here. I must go up north. Get away and think. So please give me back what's mine.'

That's what kind of bampot Guy was. He decides he wants his money back. So expects the bloke to be walking about with three hundred pounds in his hip pocket just in case Guy feels like asking for it. The Treasurer's got a terrible job convincing Guy there's not that much cash in the House. Eventually Guy believes him. 'Okay,' he says. 'How much have you got?' 'Only the shop budget,' the boy says. Every couple of months the van went someplace miles away to get more rice and queer stuff to sell in the shop. 'Right,' says Guy, 'I'll take that. You can post the rest of what you owe me to my parents' house.'

That's how Guy and me came to be walking out of the House together. Me with a couple of plastic bags full of new clothes. All dirty. And Guy looking like he owns nothing, as usual. Just the lump in the trouser pocket of his boiler suit, where the wad of notes was.

I was glad it was dry. And not cold. I hadn't been able to lift a coat anywhere yet. Halfway down the front steps Guy stops me. 'Look up!' he says. 'All those stars! Billions. Wouldn't you like to find out more about them?' I'm just standing there swinging my bags. But Guy keeps going. 'I'm going up north now,' he says. 'To a real Community. The one I should have been in all along. We could find out all about those stars there. Want to come?'

It was like you were listening to a drunk man. I didn't know where to look. Guy's grinning and birling round on the steps with his arms out. Keeping his face turned up to the sky. You can't talk to somebody on that caper. But I'd about eight pence in my pocket so I says 'I wouldn't mind.' Guy shouts out like a big ape and jumps the last six steps. 'All right!' he says. 'We're free! We'll just pop back to my parents' house for ten minutes. It's empty. They're away. I just want to get cleaned up and pack a few things. Then – we're on the road!' He slaps me on the back. I just looks the other way.

See when we walk in the door of Guy's old man's place? That's when I know he's not just an idiot. He's a nutter. You'd need to be a loony not to want to live there. Even though it's big rooms. They've got fitted carpets. Good heaters. New furniture. Colour telly. The lot. And Guy could have been living there the past six months. Instead of that he's away freezing in the dark with a bunch of headbangers. 'Have a seat,' he says to me. 'I'm just going upstairs for a bit. Won't be long. You can put the teevee on. There's fruit and chocolate and stuff on the sideboard. Make yourself at home.'

So I'm sitting there, watching a war picture, eating an apple. It's a great telly. Great colour. I switch it over and get a Western. I shove most of the box of chocolates in my pocket for after. Then I start needing the toilet. So I follow Guy up the stair.

There's water splashing behind one door. So I knock on that. 'Guy,' I says, 'I'm bursting so I am. Can I get in?' 'It's open,' he says.

You should have seen this bathroom. The size of a sitting-room. Bigger than a sitting-room. Yellow sunken bath. Wash-hand basin. Spotlights. Mirrors. Big tins of talcum powder and wee bottles of perfume. Shower cabinet up the far end with Guy in it. 'There's another toilet downstairs,' he's saying.

But I'm not listening to him.

I'm peeing. But my eyes can only see one thing. Guy's boiler suit hanging over the side of the bath.

I pulls my fly up and walks over to it. 'You going to be a while?' I says, just to keep Guy happy. But before he says a word me and the boiler suit are out the door. I shoves my fingers in the first pocket. Nothing. I shoves my fingers in the other pocket. First I can only feel the cold material. Then I feel the warm paper.

The money's still there.

The next bit's easy. That easy I can hardly believe it. Even now. I grabs the notes. I'm down the stair, out the door and in this taxi before I've time to think about it. And now I'm here. Safe. Flush. Getting driven to the station.

I know the place I'm going to get a train to. 'Scotland's Holiday Paradise'. I've always fancied taking a look at it. I'll go down there. Spend this money. That'll take a while. After it's away I'll give somebody a false name and get a job as a waiter. It's a job I've always fancied, a waiter. It ought to be easy. Hotels'll be needing workers, with the good weather coming in.

The Kitemaker'll go down to my trial. He can tell them what happened. They'll get on fine. Him and the lawyers and the cops and the posh people. They don't need me.

THE RETURN

Lorn M. Macintyre

When she left the late train at Invernevis, there was no one there to wrap welcoming arms around her and relieve her of the heavy suitcase. The hicks sitting in the sultry shadows on laundry hampers stencilled with INVERNEVIS ARMS exchanged glances and mutchkins of whisky as they watched the one arrival. One hand lugged the strapped suitcase with strange initials in the lower right corner, and the other was clasped by the child in a blue coat and matching skipped cap who scarcely came up to her thighbone. The little boy was staring at the hicks' heels kicking wicker as they drank fire from stone.

Hugh the porter (alias the bear because of the rolling gait, the result of a rogue plough) observed the needless ritual of the red flag. She was left alone on the platform with her suitcase, her son, and an empty game hamper for the big house. They called to her from the shadows under the serrated roof and she answered them in their own tongue to show that she had not forgotten. 'Se oidhche mhath a tha'nn' (it's a fine night), they said, and she did not deny it. But she wanted no crudities because the boy had their language.

She climbed the steep brae into the village, away from clinking stone and whispering. Her black hair was held back in a pony tail and her complexion the colour of the malleable dust of her profession. The green herringbone coat padded at the shoulders was too long, the black brogues too large, as if they were in danger of being left behind in the dust of a summer panting for autumn. The splay-footed action was reminiscent of the small comedian of the silent screen who had recently arrived in the Invernevis Hall, courtesy of the laird, but her short figure had Chaplin's fierce dignity.

She passed the whitewashed row of cottages which seemed to have been built for very small persons and whose neat net curtains in the squares that served as windows seemed to move as she passed. Someone greeted her in Gaelic from a low doorway, alluding to the fading sky streaked with a burst sun, and she merely nodded, going round the dormant collie. The suitcase was dragging her to one side but she was determined not to set it down until she was clear of the village. Her pace was adjusted to that of the small boy looking back at the last of the village as they began the descent into countryside. The lengthening shadows were forcing the owls to acknowledge their wakefulness in a silence suggestive of thunder.

When she reached the bottom of the long hill she set down the suitcase against the smothered milestone, the obsolete calculator of coaching days. She snapped open the brown handbag and gave him chocolate. He sat on the milestone to eat it, contemplating his first cow through rusted barbed wire as he munched, tearing away the silver paper and offering his mother a square which she refused with a hug. 'Aye, you'll beat them all for manners,' she said, but she did not say it in Gaelic. 'Now put the paper in your pocket because the Major doesn't like it lying around. Only tinkers do that.'

He didn't need a second telling. Whatever genes had collaborated in his conception had got his features right. With his chubby cheeks, brown eyes and high domed forehead he looked like a cherub, one of a strictly limited edition consistent through time. Only the large sentimental eyes seemed to have come from her. He tilted his face while she took chocolate from the corners of his mouth with a dampened handkerchief, and she hugged him again.

They moved on, through the hedges where he broke free and tried to help with the suitcase, running beside her, bruising his shins, both hands on the strap. Though he was getting in her way she did not try to stop him because her eyes and thoughts were going on ahead, up that narrow stifling tunnel of straggling hedge stopped by the mountain. It loomed large in memory, so massive that it made her legs weak. It was five years since she had taken that road in re-verse, and with the cast-offs from a disused Invernevis wardrobe (the Blue room) to conceal the fact that she was far gone with whosoever it was. She had gone through bulky hedges where the birds were building, her ankles swollen through having to carry the ever-increasing weight of her own body. She had gone with the same suitcase, the same coat to catch the dawn train to the south, having emphatically refused a lift to the next station up the line in the Major's gig.

So she went south in the spring of 1916, on a dawn train solemn with the last of Invernevis's contribution to the trenches, the young men who had preferred to see their names in writing rather than accept the King's Shilling via the Major, Boer war veteran out recruiting on the first morning of the war, knocking on croft doors with the silver butt of his riding crop and trying to conceal from the sleepy young men he had raised a leg permanently stiff with shrap-nel.

She sat in a carriage with the reluctant soldiers, her hands folded on strained herringbone, the strapped suitcase above her pony tail bouncing like a big salmon in a landing net. The recruits were too concerned with their own destinies to speculate, and if they had (even if only with their eyes) would have got no change out of her because she wasn't conscious of shame, folk memory warning that it had happened to far better than her.

The train pulled out of Invernevis, leaving puzzled faces behind static glass. Whose? The Major's? Had he heard that suggestion in the village while up for his daily supply of brandy he would have reached for the horsewhip that lay coiled by his brogues in the gig, allegedly for poachers. He had used it once in the village, for something said about the mental health of his late wife, and the people had cowered in doorways at the enormity of his presence, a cold cigar clamped in the corner of his moustached mouth and the whip flaying his own shadow as the offender cringed by the water-trough kneading his cap, asking in Gaelic for forgiveness, a language the Major did not have.

So whose? Because such questions always return to spawn. Several days before her sudden departure a footman had been dismissed, apparently for pilfering silver, and the loose-ness of his tongue (aided by the locals) in the pub before he boarded the late train suggested that he knew something. By the time the train pulled out with the inebriated servant, the father was a young man who had gone to war some months previously. But MacRitchie had died at the front, thus pre-venting the cook cum housekeeper at Invernevis from naming after him that which swelled within her. It was, as Mac-Ritchie's mother said, too clever and too wicked of her.

But where had she gone? To her relatives? She had none, except her brother Hector, the piper at the big house, and he had been the first to obey the Major's patriotic call. From time to time rumour returned by train: how she had been seen in Glasgow, in a feather hat, laughing, leaning on a man's arm in Argyle Street, and with no sign of the subject of speculation in the vicinity. Someone swore that she was cooking in a high-class restaurant where violins played. But the drunken man who insisted that she had gone on the streets had to have his mouth broken.

Wherever she had been, she was back, this time with a small boy whose clothes suggested hard work or subsidy. The war was over three years, and the granite memorial depicting the back-to-back soldiers scrutinizing the four points of the compass with fixed bayonets but empty eye sockets had been unveiled in the village by the Major. MacRitchie's name was on the long bronze plaque.

As they approached the end of the hedges the mountain loomed, the evening shadows sweeping down its sheep-studded scree. At its base Invernevis House, its whitewashed walls dulled by dusk, and the small black plantation behind where the roe-deer mustered on frosty nights. The road was following the curve of the river now, the small boy keeping close and clasping her hands because of the bats' wings brushing, like the black gloves of the elderly ladies in the Glasgow parks.

'That's where we're going,' she said, pointing.

His face betrayed the novelty and fear of childish perspective, wide river, large house, looming mountain, with the pigeons' spooky calls supplying the soundtrack.

'I want to go back to Glasgow,' he said in panic, dragging his feet in the dust.

'No,' she said, gently but firmly, keeping the suitcase moving. 'It's a nice quiet place and you'll love it. Plenty of room to play.' No more clanging trams and climbs up steep fetid stairs to a dim room.

'Who'll I play with?' he asked.

But she was not listening. They were passing that sickle of water, the Summer House pool where the Major's late wife had sat sewing while he cast, sending out strategically placed flies in search of the record salmon. She had died in a dogcart accident and the Major had married a German countess who had imposed a regime of black stockings and temperance. But the Countess had returned to her defeated land, taking Invernevis silver in her monogrammed trunks, and the Major was once again alone. The letter was in her handbag, and the train ticket used.

As they crossed Wade's hump-backed bridge thunder rumbled behind the mountain, like heavy furniture being shifted. She hurried up the twisting drive of rhododendrons, their tendons clutching herringbone, her shoes stumbling on exposed stone. The boy cowered against her as the tense sky split in deluge, drumming on the leaves. By the time the house was in sight they were sodden. Water was sounding in her shoes as they went round the ivy-stained stone to the back door.

She did not need to knock. There was fire in the big grate and the white table was scrubbed. She stepped out of her shoes and tilted them on the hearth, having helped the boy from his dripping coat.

'A nice cup of tea,' she said, putting the kettle on bright coal.

It was as she had left it five years before on the morning she had removed the embarrassment from the big house. It was as if the same coals had been spreading heat without diminishing for five years; as if hissing bristle under her fist had only that morning scrubbed the white board. She opened a press and shook out a starched overall, sitting the child at the end of the table with two cushions propped under him to raise him to the level of the cup of tea.

'You need your bed,' she said, filling the kettle, and (without having to think) taking the stone bottle down.

'Mummy!'

She turned to see the Major standing in the doorway, an old cigar between two fingers. His failure to come forward and shake hands after five years had nothing to do with a lack of manners or the decanter of brandy he had already consumed, though the evening was still young, with more feathers to be snipped, to conceal the bare hook.

'A nasty night,' he murmured as he patted the small boy's head. 'And what's *your* name?'

'John – sir,' he said meekly, conscious that his mother was watching him.

'Good. That's one of mine.'

He was older, of course, and his face had set in the colour of decayed salmon flesh because of his brandy consumption.

But he was still a fine-looking man, she thought, despite the game leg, the frayed tweeds buttressed by leather.

'I'll get your dinner, sir,' she said.

'There's cold salmon in the larder,' he said. 'But put the boy to bed first.'

She carried him upstairs. The single bed in the neat but spartan room with ewer and basin on mottled marble was as she had left it. She stripped and settled him, putting in the hot stone and leaving a small lamp burning, for the first few nights at least, though he hadn't asked.

The room was strange and eerie, and he didn't like the way the dark wood absorbed the light. But he was tired after the long journey. The stone shared its heat, and the river quickened by torrent was more pleasant than clanging trams.

If it was the Major's, it was never said. It would have been transmitted in a glance, and if she had been dicing vegetables when he came in to suggest that she go away for a time, the knife would not have skidded, wounding. And if on a summer's night of derisory owls the Major, pining for his first wife after his first decanter, and convinced of his strength despite cirrhosis (that hook in the side), had gripped the fluted stem of the heavy glass lamp to take the back stairs and cast his long shadow – but no, some things are private.

And the boy? If he displayed some mental promise some trust fund would be tapped to send him to university. But he would never sit at the big table out front, and the Major would always be *sir*.

And Maggie? She was back, as if she had only stepped out for a minute to talk to the tinkers, leaving the slow dough rising in the oven.

PASS BY THE OBSERVATORY

Alan Mason

When I was in the country last summer, I circled the occasional gazebo with a couple of charming women, who had
all the wit and beauty one could desire in female companions,
with a dash of coquetry, that from time to time gave me a
great many agreeable torments. I was, after my way, in love
with both of them, and had such frequent opportunities of
pleading my passion to one or the other when they were
asunder, that I had reason to hope for particular favours from
each. One evening I was privately recalling my unnecessary
departure from North Africa a few years previously; I was
standing by the window, with nothing about me but my
night-gown, when the two ladies came into my chamber and
informed me of a very pleasant trick they wished to put upon
a gentleman that was in the house, provided I would bear a
part in it. Upon this they told me such a plausible story, that
I laughed at their contrivance and agreed to do whatever they
should require of me. They immediately began to swaddle me
up in my night-gown, with long pieces of linen, which they
folded about me till they had wrapped my body in above a
hundred yards of swath. My arms were pressed to my sides,
and my legs closed together by so many wrappers one over
another, that I looked like an Egyptian mummy. As I stood
bolt-upright upon one end in this antique figure, one of the
ladies burst out a-laughing. 'And now, Kleiser,' says she, 'we
intend to perform the promise that we find you have extorted
from each of us, and I dare say you are a better-bred cavalier
than to refuse to go to bed to two ladies that desire it of you.'
After having stood a fit of laughter, I begged them to uncase

me, and to do with me what they pleased. 'No, no,' said they, 'we like you very well as you are,' and upon that ordered me to be carried to one of their houses, and put to bed in all my swaddles. The room was lighted upon all sides: and I was laid very decently between a pair of sheets, with my head (which was indeed the only part I could move) upon a very high pillow: this was no sooner done, but my two female friends came into bed with me in their finest night-clothes. You may easily guess at the condition of a man that saw a couple of the most beautiful women in the world undressed and a-bed with him, without being able to stir hand or foot. I begged them to release me, and struggled all I could to get loose, which I did with so much violence, that about midnight, they both leaped out of the bed, crying out they were undone. But seeing me safe, they took their posts again, and renewed their raillery. Finding all my prayers and endeavours were lost, I composed myself as well as I could, and told them that if they would not unbind me, I would fall asleep between them, and by that means disgrace them for ever. But, alas! this was impossible; could I have been disposed to it, they would have prevented me by several little ill-natured caresses and endearments which they bestowed upon me. As much devoted as I am to womankind, I would not pass such another night to be master of the whole sex. My reader will doubtless be curious to know what became of me the next morning. Why truly my bed-fellows left me about an hour before day, and told me, if I would be good and lie still, they would send somebody to take me up as soon as it was time for me to rise. Accordingly about nine o'clock in the morning I fell asleep.

I have looked over the minutes of the dream which I composed while in this state, and now, without further preface, I shall enter upon an exact relation of it:

I was invited, methought, along with several colleagues, to the dissection of a coquette's heart.

Our operator, before he engaged in this visionary dissection, told us that there was nothing in his art more difficult than to lay open the heart of a coquette, by reason of the many labyrinths and recesses which are to be found in it, and which do not appear in the heart of any other animal.

He desired us first of all to observe the pericardium, or outward case of the heart, which we did very attentively; and by the help of our glasses discerned in it millions of little sears, which seem to have been occasioned by the points of innumerable darts and arrows, that from time to time had glanced upon the outward coat; though we could not discover the smallest orifice, by which any of them had entered and pierced the inward substance.

Every smatterer in anatomy knows that this pericardium, or case of the heart, contains in it a thin reddish liquor, supposed to be bred from the vapours which exhale out of the heart, and being stopped here, are condensed into this watery substance. Upon examining this liquor, we found that it had in it all the qualities of that spirit which is made use of in the thermometer, to show the change of weather.

Nor must I here omit an experiment one of the company assured us he himself had made with this liquor, which he found in great quantity about the heart of a coquette whom he had formerly dissected. He affirmed to us, that he had actually enclosed it in a small tube made after the manner of a weather-glass; but that instead of acquainting him with the varieties of the atmosphere, it showed him the qualities of those persons who entered the room where it stood. He affirmed also, that it rose at the approach of a plume of feathers, an embroidered coat, or a pair of fringed gloves; and that it fell as soon as an ill-shaped periwig, a clumsy pair of shoes, or an unfashionable coat came into his house. Nay, he proceeded so far as to assure us, that upon his laughing aloud when he stood by it, the liquor mounted very sensibly, and immediately sunk again upon his looking serious. In short, he told us, that he knew very well, by this invention, whenever he had a man of sense or a coxcomb in his room.

Having cleared away the pericardium, or the case, and liquor above-mentioned, we came to the heart itself. The outward surface of it was extremely slippery, and the mucro, or point, so very cold withal, that upon endeavouring to take hold of it, it glided through the fingers like a smooth piece of ice.

The fibres were turned and twisted in a more intricate and perplexed manner than they are usually found in other hearts; insomuch that the whole heart was wound up together in a Gordian knot, and must have had very irregular and unequal motions, while it was employed in its vital function.

One thing we thought very observable, namely, that upon examining all the vessels which came into it, or issued out of it, we could not discover any communication that it had with the tongue.

We could not but take notice likewise, that several of those little nerves in the heart which are affected by the sentiments of love, hatred, and other passions, did not descend to this before us from the brain, but from the muscles which lie about the eye.

Upon weighing the heart in my hand, I found it to be extremely light, and consequently very hollow, which I did not wonder at, when, upon looking into the inside of it, I saw multitudes of cells or cavities, running one within another as our historians describe the apartments of Rosamond's bower. Several of these little hollows were stuffed with innumerable sorts of trifles, which I shall forbear giving any particular account of, and shall therefore only take notice of what lay first and uppermost, which upon our unfolding it, and applying our microscopes to it, appeared to be a flame-coloured hood.

We are informed that the lady of this heart, when living, received the addresses of several who made love to her, and did not only give each of them encouragement, but made every one she conversed with believe that she regarded him with an eye of kindness; for which reason we expected to have seen the impressions of multitudes of faces among the several plaits and foldings of the heart; but to our great surprise, not a single print of this nature discovered itself until we came into the very core and centre of it. We there observed a little figure, which, upon applying our glasses to it, the more I thought I had seen the face before, but could not possibly recollect either the place or time; when at length, one of the company, who had examined this figure more nicely than the rest, showed us plainly by the make of its face, and the several turns of its features, that the little idol which was thus lodged in the very middle of the heart was a deceased beau whom we had all once known very well.

As soon as we had finished our dissection, we resolved to make an experiment of the heart, not being able to determine among ourselves the nature of its substance, which differed in so many particulars from that of the heart in other females. Accordingly we laid it in a pan of burning coals, when we observed in it a certain salamandrine quality, that made it capable of living in the midst of fire and flame, without being consumed, or so much as singed.

As we were admiring this strange phenomenon, and standing round the heart in a circle, it gave a most prodigious sigh, or rather crack, and dispersed all at once in smoke and vapour. This imaginary noise, which methought was louder than the burst of a cannon, produced such a violent shake in my brain, that it dissipated the fumes of sleep and left me in an instant broad awake.

Had I slept all day? Still wrapped and trapped in my linen dilemma I awoke in darkness to find myself seated in a tub among the ruins of an old abbey. When and why had the ladies, or their servants, deposited me in this dismal place? For I could not but fancy it one of the most proper scenes in

the world for a ghost to appear in. The tub did nothing to re-
assure me; indeed, I was only too glad to squirm and stumble
an inelegant escape from its dry dip. As I hopped in my cocoon
past burying places and aged elms (the dusk of the evening
conspiring with so many other occasions of terror) I observed
a cow grazing not far from me, which an imagination that was
apt to startle might easily have construed into, say, a black
horse without a head.

There is no kind of exercise which I would so recommend
to my readers of both sexes as this of bouncing across
treacherous, slippy and irregular countryside in the middle of
the night, while emptying lungs of abuse at the heavens; all
this in the desperate hope of summoning into existence a
warm house, and a well-disposed host who might possess a
sharp knife or a good pair of scissors. For my own part, when
I am in town, for want of these opportunities, I exercise myself an hour every morning upon a dumb bell that is placed in
a corner of my room, and it pleases me the more because it
does everything I require of it in the most profound silence.
My landlady and her daughters are so well acquainted with
my hours of exercise, that they never come into my room to
disturb me whilst I am ringing.

The first eye of consequence (under the invisible Author of
all) is the invisible luminary of the universe. This glorious
spectator is said never to open his eyes at his rising in a
morning, without having a whole kingdom of adorers in
Persian silk waiting at his levee. Millions of creatures derive
their sight from this original, who besides his being the great
director of optics, is the surest test whether eyes be of the
same species with that of an eagle, or that of an owl. The one
he emboldens with a manly assurance to look, speak, act, or
plead, before the faces of a numerous assembly; the other he
dazzles out of countenance into a sheepish dejectedness. The
sun-proof eye dares lead up a dance in a full court: and with-

out blinking at the lustre of beauty, can distribute an eye of proper complaisance to a room crowded with company, each of which deserves particular regard; while the other sneaks from conversation, like a fearful debtor who never dares to look out, but when he can see nobody, and nobody him.

It was the most bright morning; and I stood wearily upon an expansive heath, finally bruised beneath my bandages. Hazy sportsmen had been beating the scrub-land for some time, when, as I was at a little distance from the rest of the company, I saw a hare pop out from a small furze-brake almost under my tied feet. I marked the way she took, which I endeavoured to make the huntsmen sensible of by extending my neck and pointing my head in the proper direction; but to no purpose, till a man who realized that my extraordinary motions were significant, rode up to me and asked me if puss was gone that way? Upon my answering yes, he immediately called in the dogs, and put them upon the scent. As they were going off, I heard one of the country fellows muttering to his companion, 'that 'twas a wonder they had not lost all their sport, for want of the silent gentleman parcel crying, Stole away.'

This, with my aversion to leaping hedges, made me withdraw to a rising ground, from whence I could have the pleasure of the whole chase, without the fatigue of keeping up with the hounds. The hare immediately threw them above a mile behind her; but I was pleased to find, instead of running straight forwards, or, in hunter's language 'flying the country', as I was afraid she might have done, she wheeled about, and described a sort of circle round the hill where I had taken my station, in such a manner as gave me a very distinct view of the sport. I could see her first pass by, and the dogs some time afterwards, unravelling the whole track she had made, and following her through all her doubles. I was at the same time delighted in observing that deference which the rest of the pack paid to each particular hound, according to the character he had acquired among them. If they were at fault, and an old hound of reputation opened but once, he was immediately followed by the whole cry; while a raw dog, or one who was a noted liar, might have yelped his heart out, without being taken notice of.

The hare now, after having squatted two or three times, and being put up again as often, came still nearer to the place where she was at first started. The dogs pursued her, and these were followed by a jolly knight (at least I dubbed him so), who rode upon a white gelding, encompassed by his tenants and servants. One of the sportsmen rode up to me and told me that he was sure the chase was almost at an end, because the old dogs, which had hitherto lain behind, now headed the pack. The fellow was in the right. Our hare took a large field just under us, followed by the full cry in view. I must confess the brightness of the weather, the cheerfulness of everything around me, the chiding of the hounds, which was returned upon us in a double echo from two neighbouring hills, with the hallooing of the sportsmen, and the sounding of the horn, lifted my spirits to such an extent that I felt compelled to scratch my thighs with the ends of my fingers, this being the only hobby I had mastered since my incarceration. If I was under any concern, it was on account of the poor hare, that was now quite spent, and almost within the reach of her enemies; when the huntsman getting forward, threw down his pole before the dogs. They were now within eight yards of that game which they had been pursuing for almost as many hours; yet on the signal before-mentioned they all made a sudden stand, and though they continued opening as much as before, durst not once attempt to pass beyond the pole. At the same time the knight rode forward, and alighting, took up the hare in his arms; which he soon after delivered up to one of his servants with an order if she could be kept alive, to let her go in his great orchard; where it seems he has several of these prisoners of war, who live together in a very comfortable

captivity. I was highly pleased to see the discipline of the
pack, and the good nature of the knight, who could not find it
in his heart to murder a creature that had given him so much
diversion.

Surprise is so much the life of stories, that everyone aims at it
who endeavours to please by telling them. Smooth delivery,
an elegant choice of words and a sweet arrangement, are all
beautifying graces but not the particulars in this point of conversation which either long command the attention, or strike
with the violence of a sudden passion, or occasion the burst
of laughter which accompanies humour. I have sometimes
fancied that the mind is in this case like a traveller who sees a
fine seat in haste; he acknowledges the delightfulness of a walk
set with regularity, but would be uneasy if he were to pace it
over, when the first view had let him into all its beauties from
one end to the other.

However, a knowledge of the success which stories will have
when they are attended with a turn of surprise, as it has
happily made the characters of some, so it has also been the
ruin of the characters of others. There is a set of men who
outrage truth, instead of affecting us with a manner in telling
it; who overleap the line of probability, that they may be seen
to move out of the common road; and endeavour only to make
their hearers stare by imposing upon them with a kind of
nonsense against the philosophy of nature, or such a heap of
wonders told upon their own knowledge, as it is not likely one
man should have ever met with.

I have been led to this observation by the company of
sportsmen into which I fell accidentally. The subject of
antipathies was a proper field wherein such false surprises
might expatiate, and there were those present who appeared
very fond to show it in its full extent of traditional history.
Some of them, in a learned manner, offered to our consideration the miraculous powers which the effluviums of cheese

have over bodies whose pores are disposed to receive them in a noxious manner; others gave an account of such who could indeed bear the sight of cheese, but not the taste; for which they brought a reason from the milk of their nurses. Others again discoursed, without endeavouring at reasons, concerning an unconquerable aversion which some stomachs have against a joint of meat when it is whole, and the eager inclination they have for it when, by its being cut up, the shape which had affected them is altered. From hence they passed to eels, then to parsnips, and so from one aversion to another, until we had worked ourselves to such a pitch of complaisance that when the dinner was to come in, we inquired the name of every dish and hoped it would be no offence to any company before it was admitted. When we had sat down, this civility among us turned the discourse from eatables to other sorts of aversions; and the eternal cat, which plagues every conversation of this nature, began then to engross the subject. One had sweated at the sight of it, another had smelled it out as it lay concealed in a very distant cupboard; and he who crowned the whole set of these stories, reckoned up the number of times in which it had occasioned him to swoon away. 'At last,' says he, 'that you may all be satisfied of my invincible aversion to a cat, I shall give an unanswerable instance. As I was going through a street of London, where I had never been until then, I felt a general damp and faintness all over me, which I could not tell how to account for, until I chanced to cast my eyes upwards, and found that I was passing under a sign-post on which the picture of a cat was hung.'

The extravagance of this turn in the way of surprise gave a stop to the talk we had been carrying on. Some were silent because they doubted, and others because they were conquered in their own way; so that the gentleman had an opportunity to press the belief of it upon us, and let us see that he was rather exposing himself than ridiculing others.

I must freely own that I did not all this while disbelieve

everything that was said; but yet I thought some in the company had been endeavouring who should pitch the bar furthest; that it had for some time been a measuring cast, and at last my friend of the cat and sign-post had thrown beyond them all.

I then considered the manner in which this story had been received, and the possibility that it might have passed for a jest upon others, if he had not laboured against himself. From hence, thought I, there are two ways which the well-bred world gentleman takes to correct such a practice, when they do not think fit to contradict it flatly.

The first of these is a general silence, which I would not advise anyone to interpret in his own behalf. It is often the effect of prudence in avoiding a quarrel, when they see another drive so fast that there is no stopping him without being run against; and but very seldom the effect of weakness in believing suddenly. The generality of mankind are not so grossly ignorant, as some overbearing spirits would persuade themselves; and if the authority of a character or a caution against danger make us suppress our opinions, yet neither of these are of force enough to suppress our thoughts of them. If a man who has endeavoured to amuse his company with improbabilities could but look into their minds, he would find that they imagine he lightly esteems of their sense when he thinks to impose upon them, and that he is less esteemed by them in his attempt in doing so. His endeavour to glory at their expense becomes a ground of quarrel, and the scorn and indifference with which they entertain it begins the immediate punishment: and indeed (if we should even go no further) silence, or a negligent indifference, has a deeper way of wounding than opposition, because opposition proceeds from an anger that has a sort of generous sentiment for the adversary mingling along with it, while it shows that there is some esteem in your mind for him: in short, that you think him worthwhile to contest with. But silence, or negligent indifference, proceeds from anger, mixed with scorn that shows another he is thought by you too contemptible to be regarded.

The other method which the world has taken for correcting this practice of false surprise, is to overshoot such talkers in their own bow, or to raise the story with further degrees of impossibility, and set up for a voucher to them in such a manner as must let them see they stand detected. Thus I have heard a discourse was once managed upon the effects of fear. One of the company had given an account how it had turned his friend's hair grey in a night, while the terrors of a shipwreck encompassed him. Another, taking the hint from hence, began upon his own knowledge to enlarge his instances of the like nature to such a number, that it was not probable he could ever have met with them: and as he still grounded these upon different causes for the sake of variety, it might seem at last, from his share of the conversation, almost impossible that anyone who can feel the passion of fear should all his life escape so common an effect of it. By this time, some of the company grew negligent, or desirous to contradict him: but one rebuked the rest with an appearance of severity, and, with the known old story in his head, assured them they need not scruple to believe that the fear of anything can make a man's hair grey, since he knew one whose periwig had suffered so by it. Thus he stopped the talk, and made them easy. Thus is the same method taken to bring us to shame, which we fondly take to increase our character. It is indeed a kind of mimicry, by which another puts on our air of conversation to show us to ourselves. He seems to look ridiculous before, that you may remember how near a resemblance you bear to him, or that you may know he will not lie under the imputation of believing you. Then it is that you are struck dumb immediately with a conscientious shame for what you have been saying. Then it is that you are inwardly grieved at the sentiments which you cannot but perceive others entertain concerning you. In short, you are against yourself; the laugh of the company runs against you; the censuring world is obliged to you for that triumph which you have allowed them at your expense; and truth, which you have injured, has a near way of being revenged on you, when by the bare repetition of your story, you become a frequent diversion for the public.

THE BUNDLING

Alanna Knight

Towards the end of the last century, there lived in Sollas a
girl whose beauty and sweet nature were cause for jubilation
among her family and friends. Her name was Isabella. She
was sixteen, the sweetheart of Iain, a handsome youth whose
home lay ten miles distant, across treacherous moor and peatbog.

Since Isabella's parents' croft was crowded by young and
old, animal and human, bed was the only warm and private
place for lovers and the problem of courtship was solved by
the time honoured custom of 'bundling'. Laid side by side
for the night, all attempts at greater intimacies than kissing
and loving words were frustrated by the sacks into which the
couple were individually – and securely – sewn by the girl's
mother. After a year and a day of such courtship, it was considered that they knew each other and their own minds well
enough to enjoy a more complete consummation. Both being
agreeable, their nuptials were accordingly arranged.

The wedding day dawned fine and clear. The minister
was rowed across to Lochmaddy and thence by cart to Sollas
where Isabella, in her bridal gown, radiantly awaited the
arrival of the bridegroom's party from across the moor.

No exact time had been appointed for the ceremony. 'Being
late' belonged to a more sophisticated society and had not yet
been invented on the island. The leisurely probing of auld
acquaintance, the taking of drams, the delicious exchange of
gossip were conducted according to island custom and eti-
quette and calculated to extend over many hours. It was not
until the minister – a mainland man, whose ignorance could

be excused – showed some impatience by consulting his watch with anxious glances and hints about catching the evening tide, that the laughter and gaiety thinned a little. Looks and whispers were exchanged among the bride's party and in ones and twos, they went outside, to 'take a look down-by'.

After several such excursions, someone spotted the bridegroom's party as a distant column threading its way across the moor. The bride and her maids were hastily reassembled, hair combed and dresses straightened. The flushed countenances of the men were hurriedly doused with cold water into a semblance of sobriety. Then all were hustled or supported – according to their needs, into the church and down the aisle, there to be seen waiting decorously, eyes modestly lowered, before the altar.

A little time elapsed before the bridegroom's party puffed its way up the last steep brae.

'And where is Iain?' demanded Isabella's mother.

'He is with you,' said Iain's father.

'He is not. He went back to you.'

There was some uneasiness when it was discovered that Iain had not been seen since leaving Isabella's croft two mornings earlier to assemble his family and return with them for the wedding. There were wry smiles and no real alarm as yet. It was well-known that a prospective bridegroom's progress was subject to the exigencies of too many drams taken.

'He will be sleeping it off somewhere,' said his elder brother Andrew.

'But we have brought his wedding braws with us,' said his mother.

'Where is Iain?' said the bride, who, tired of waiting, had come out of the church, still clutching her bouquet of fast-wilting flowers. Her mother took her aside and questioned her closely about her parting with Iain.

'Was all well between you? There was no quarrel?'

'Never – never.'

Iain's bachelor friends were overheard whispering that perhaps he had changed his mind, lost his nerve. This was hotly denied by his family who knew him to be a solid un-imaginative lad, keen for the shackles of matrimony. And despite those exceptional good looks, he had never to their certain knowledge chased other girls.

Tearfully now, Isabella recalled his departure from the croft, her mother nodding agreement to each and every detail.

'Did he intend calling on friends?' asked Iain's father.

'Yes – think hard. Some invitation to the wedding he wanted to deliver himself – a last-minute guest who had been overlooked?'

'Doubtless he was offered a dram too many,' said the cynical Andrew.

'No.' Both Isabella and her mother were unshakable in that Iain had declared he was heading straight home. And all agreed that Iain was not an intemperate drinker, by island standards.

'A wise head, sensible-like on those young shoulders of his,' sighed his mother.

'Aye, and a keen sense of responsibility – and for what is proper,' said his father.

'Besides,' added the young bachelors, 'no bridegroom in his right senses could be expected to miss his wedding Ceilidh.'

At this juncture Isabella's neighbour recalled seeing Iain leaving the croft. She had been watching for her own man returning from the fishing and recalled the heavy mist. 'I was anxious, for it lay like a shroud all around us.'

The memory prompted others: 'Now you mention it – our boat lay off the shore most of the day.'

'Aye, and when I went out to the byre, I could hardly see

my hand on the milking pail.'

Now Isabella and her mother remembered that mist and fear took the place of their anger and humiliation.

'Such weather is not unusual for May.'

'Man, these May fogs are notorious.'

Notorious, common, the weather had not been given a second thought in the account of Iain's mysterious disappearance. Now it seemed with appalling significance, Iain's father suggested: 'I think it would be well in the circumstances if we organized a search party.' When Isabella cried out, he said consolingly: 'No need to worry yourself. He cannot be far away. We will doubtless be finding him with a sprained ankle or something of the sort – '

To Isabella, her mother and everyone else, it sounded a forlorn hope, but the wedding guests brightened, took on a few more drams and cheerful faces, just to keep up her spirits. All that day and night the men searched. They were experienced in such matters, accustomed to beasts straying, so their efficiency was never in doubt.

They searched every yard of the ten miles between the two crofts, calling his name, but there was no trace of his presence and only the startled cry of sea-birds disturbed, came for answer. Occasionally they stopped for breath and exchanged frightened glances, for it was indeed as if Iain had been spirited away by the little folk themselves. When at last they stumbled exhausted into Sollas, they would have welcomed any sign of the missing bridegroom – alive or dead. It was just too uncanny by far, with not even a boat gone to account for a logical explanation like drowning. Although they told each other and Isabella: 'There is naught to fret over. A simple explanation – you will see how it is. Very soon Iain will reappear and everyone will laugh and take a dram with him – '

Days passed into weeks, weeks into months until a year later, the mysterious disappearance still remained unsolved. By this time, like the heroines of grand opera – the plot of which this little melodrama somewhat resembles – poor Isabella sat huddled by the peat fire, hugging her knees, rocking back and forth and going quietly mad with grief.

'Better to be dead, the poor lass,' said those who watched the beautiful Isabella disappear into the strange twilight world of unreason, and a frail old woman, known to all as Daft Bella, emerge to take her place. Daft Bella was harmless and kindly, her frustrated years of maternity devoted tirelessly to lost animals or any small child prepared to listen patiently to her silly endearing nonsense. However, as nursemaid she proved unreliable since lucidity would peter out without warning and abandoning her charge she would be off over the heather to watch for her Iain returning.

Take a leap across time of fifty years to *Là Buidhe Bealltuinn*, the pagan May Day festival of the Yellow Day of the Fires of Bel, celebrated throughout the Hebrides by the extinguishing of all hearth fires and their relighting from sacred embers of the sacrificial fires which had burned all day on the hilltops, with cattle and livestock driven between the purifying flames.

'O God, kindle in my heart
A glimmer of the sun's warmth towards my neighbour,
Towards my enemy, towards my kindred, towards my friend,
Towards the free, towards the slave, towards the bondsman –'

On the newly opened peatfield, the women chant the *Beannachadhe Beothaidh*, the Blessing of the Kindling, as they work:

'O Sons of the Earth soft and fair,
From the lowest created thing
Up to the Circle Most High – '

The singing is cut short by a shrill scream from one of the

women. Shocked into speechlessness, she can only point a wavering finger at the peatbog.

From among the rushes rises a man's hand, ghostly and white. The men are summoned, discover there is an arm attached to the hand and that the whole adds up to the corpse of a young man. What clothes remain on his body are mere shreds, but these are the only signs of violence. There are no marks, no immediate evidence of foul play. His face is peaceful, eyes closed as if death were but a dreamless sleep and very recent.

'How did he get here? He is not one of this parish.'

And a shiver goes round the assembled group. Thoughtful but shifty glances are exchanged with neighbours. Who is this man? There is no news of any stranger in Sollas, where each new arrival immediately becomes public property, his progress a matter of speculation and interest, to be avidly reported and commented upon in hopes that someone is planning a Ceilidh in his honour.

Now the same dreadful thought slides into all minds. 'I doubt he did not die of natural causes,' says one. 'Nor of old age,' adds another, with an uneasy try at humour.

'I doubt someone murdered him on another island and rowed him over here at the dead of night, hoping the peatbog would hide him – '

'And since it did not, then the blame would lie at our doors.'

A God-fearing community, they are entitled to indignation, since there has not been one serious crime, nothing worse than broken heads in a drunken brawl, within living memory.

The minister arrives and murmurs a prayer over the corpse laid upon a trestle in the newly-built church hall.

'Shall we lay him out decently, minister?' ask the old women who take pride in such tasks.

'No. Send for the fiscal and touch nothing until he comes,' orders the minister.

'But what can he do?' Fiscal is a frightening word to those for whom breaking the law is a new experience. 'We have done nothing wrong, minister.'

'The fiscal will know if there are any missing persons from the other islands. Perhaps one who answers this young man's description.' Privately, however, the minister is entertaining grave doubts about the truthfulness of his little flock. Eyeing them narrowly he suspects that his sermons on the Ten Commandments have fallen on one pair of deaf ears, and that someone regarding him wears the brand of Cain.

By now, there is a queue two deep inside, word having circulated with uncanny speed. Carts are filling with astonishing rapidity across the island and bowling towards the church hall. Quite small children are acting as couriers, being shrilly despatched to spread the tidings to ancient grannies, uncles, aunts and second cousins who may not have heard. Everyone, it seems, is hell-bent on having a look at the corpse. No one is afraid of a dead man, since death is such a frequent visitor in most crofts as to be an almost too familiar acquaintance. Now even the smallest children shout:

'Lift me up. Let me see – I want a look at the corpse.'

They know all about death and since babyhood have witnessed both his arrival and departure, taking not only toothless doddering grandparents, but warm beloved mothers, drowned fathers and frequently little ones like themselves, playmates – and many a stillborn sibling, blue and shrivelled as a monkey.

Besides, this is a corpse with a difference. A stranger with a mystery – the hint of a crime committed. The women, ignoring the minister have, for decency's sake, tidied him up. In the removal of some of the peat, they stand back to admire their work and are immediately struck by his exceptional looks.

'Now, who would want to hurt that bonny lad, since he has the looks of an honest man, even in death – '

'Let me pass, let me pass.' A bent old woman scatters them out of her path to stare down at the trestle. Scream upon scream rings through the hall. And there is Daft Bella, clawing at the corpse, crying:

'Iain, oh Iain, *ghraidh mo chridhe* – love of my heart – '

Drawing their headshawls closer, the older women discover what has been twitching the chord of memory – the corpse resembles the missing bridegroom. Which, in fact, he is.

The minister is again summoned. A party is despatched to Iain's township with details of the discovery. On the following day they return with Iain's elder brother Andrew, his wife Dorothy. The police and fiscal arrive, ask: 'Is this your missing brother, sir?'

Andrew looks at the corpse and weeps. Dorothy clings to his arm and weeps. Andrew remembers that the missing bridegroom had a bride. Dorothy cannot remember her name and prays silently that she is dead also while Andrew hopes they will be spared the embarrassment of a confrontation with that ill-fated bride. Dorothy shies away like a frightened mare from such a meeting, knowing that they will both be old women – unrecognizable to each other. There is no escape. Daft Bella is sent for.

Meanwhile the business of death proceeds with decorum. The fiscal produces a doctor who produces a death certificate and declares the remarkable freshness of the fifty-year-old corpse is due to some mysterious preservative, contained in the peatbog. Andrew is required to set his name to certain documents and when questioned says yes, he supposes that his brother should be taken back to his own parish for burial there. 'But first, we must speak with Isabella.'

'Yes,' says his wife, 'and offer our condolences.' The words ring a hollow note. How does one offer condolences half a century too late?

A middle-aged man who was not born at the time of Iain's

disappearance rushes in. He is Hamish, Daft Bella's nephew. 'It is too late for you to meet my aunt. We found her dead in her chair. It was the shock, I expect.'

'Poor Isabella,' sighs Dorothy.

And away at the back of the hall, someone too young to know the old woman by any other name than Daft Bella, sniggers and is hushed severely into silence.

'Do you still wish to pay your respects to – her?' asks Hamish.

Dorothy gives Andrew a warning nudge. She wants to go home now, feeling that she has done her duty by horrors for today. Andrew shakes his head obedient to her wishes, disappointing some and offending others present by his failure to comply with the time-honoured custom of paying one's respects to the newly departed, especially when the deceased is related by marriage – almost.

Then Dorothy has a brilliant idea. A mainland woman, born and bred, the refinements of island life mean little to her. She knows only that her husband's brother's burial will mean an inevitable Ceilidh and a Ceilidh inevitably means expense. She does not feel in the least inclined for either or both events, especially since they have moved up in the social world with a doctor son due from Glasgow with his well-born rich wife.

'Don't you think,' she asks, 'don't you all think it would be rather *nice* if Iain could stay here with his Isabella? If they could – rest – together for all eternity?'

Everyone thinks this is a lovely sensitive suggestion and Dorothy is regarded approvingly by all but some of the children present who see more deeply into adult minds than they are given credit for. Quick to scent falsity, they stare relentlessly up into the woman's face, as if her selfish motives are clearly written there for all present to read. Dorothy blushes and takes refuge in pious weeping, while Andrew agrees to return in time for the funeral.

Carefully folded away in a chest, the old women find Isabella's wedding dress. Yellowed with age, she has kept it to be her shroud and a great deal of tugging, cutting and pinning is necessary to accommodate the now shapeless body, once so lissom. A more conventional shroud is produced for Iain and the long-ago lovers are placed in one large coffin, to lie in state in the church hall.

'A dram to speed them on their way?' hiccups the local drunk, who has just staggered in, hopeful as always, for a Ceilidh.

Silently they stare down at the ugly old woman and her young lover whose brief sojourn back in the land of the living has already attacked his once beautiful countenance with alarming signs of speedy deterioration. Upon the surrounding air hangs an ominous sweetness, not entirely due to the floral tributes. It turns the thought of a wake into an obscenity and the band of mourners drift quietly homewards.

As the last footfall fades, the hall is empty of all but the lovers. Peacefully, side by side, they lie together, after half a century apart, bundled again.

HOLY TERRORS

Anne Turner

In the heatwave, the birds grow sleeker and cheekier but the park loses its gloss. Hedges and trees grow grey under a film of fine dust. Expansive lawns turn to straw under relays of sunbathers, and litter blows past in staring colours making the roses pale in their sandy beds. The pond suffers most of all, a lukewarm jelly of weed, bread and sunken newspaper. Torpid ducks float in circles or labour up the threadbare verge. A swan sleeps it out in the shade of some tangled shrubs, and the tree on the tiny island is beaded with the slate-blue bosoms of drowsy pigeons. High on the crown of the tree, a white seagull perches like a weathervane on one thin leg.

Across the metalled road that encircles the pond, the park benches support six citizens apiece, elbow to elbow. These are the elderly, the obese and the better-dressed sunworshippers. From time to time, a paper bag rustles and bread is crumbled on to the road. Sparrows whirr down, their energies unaffected by the heat. A cloud of pigeons rises from the central tree and descends with eager burblings – but the sparrows are too quick. The crumbs soar away, airborne on gleeful beaks. Pigeons stab at the bare tarmac and, growing bored, startle themselves aloft again. The seagull, dazzling white, takes no heed.

'Lookit!'

Eight or ten noisy little boys in dirty jerseys and frayed serge shorts run forward, clawing at the railing round the pond. The pigeons rise with clapping wings, and the lethargic assembly on the benches watches with resignation as the intruders jostle and point and converse in piercing cries. The ducks change course and move off at speed, ringed by glassy eddies. The seagull stirs and unfolds the other leg. One scarecrow of a child pulls something from under his jersey and with a quick movement sends a missile spurting across the pond. It sends up a little fountain as it drops just short of the island.

Shouts of 'Aw the shame!' and 'Missed it!' mingle with raucous comments.

The boy aims again, the rowdy encouragement increases, and another missile flies wildly into the air, disappearing among the island's spindly shrubs. The swan uncurls its long neck, breasts the water and floats away until the island hides it from sight. The boys argue. They swirl around the unsuccessful sharpshooter like midges. They wave out-at-elbows arms and hop and kick and punch each other in the effort to have their say. Then a decision appears to be reached. The argument subsides and a second marksman takes his stance close to the railings.

'You wee murderers!'

The cry comes from an elderly lady in a mauve coat and hat who rises, stout and breathless, from her place on a bench. Her companion, older and hunched in black, rises too. The boys squirm down from the railings, close ranks, and eye the angry women warily. The piercing voices falter and turn to hoarse whispers. The mauve lady bustles over to them, her plump face flushed and vengeful.

'And what do you think you're doing?' she demands, raising her handbag and shaking it threateningly.

The boys stand firm and set up a clamour of explanation. They all shout out at once so that not a word can be understood. They jerk thumbs over shoulders at the pond, gabbling in a vernacular as turbid as the water. The woman glances at her older friend who shrugs in sour bafflement.

'You – ' The stout lady fixes on the marksman. 'Was that a

155

catapult I saw? Were you shooting stones at the wee birds?'

The accusation sets the boys dancing in an agony of denial. 'Naw. No' the birds!' they shout, shaking their heads virtuously. They appeal to one another's authority, and continue to pour out a torrent of explanations.

The women are taken aback. They are used to sly mischief and bad language, and this is neither. Though they can hardly understand a word, they recognize right-minded indignation on every grimy face.

'If they'd just speak one at a time – !' exclaims the older lady, looking upset.

The other lady will not be put off. 'Give me the catapult!' She holds out a hand. 'D'you hear?'

'It's no' mines,' says the boy, stepping back a pace and clutching the front of his jersey where the weapon is hidden. 'It's his – he gie'd me it!' His hand jerks at the tallest, skinniest lad, who is at once surrounded by protectors.

'I don't care whose it is,' the lady insists. 'You're not throwing stones at the birds here.'

'A good hiding, the lot of you,' mutters the old lady uneasily. There is growing concern on her shrivelled face as she looks from one pallid urchin to another. Memories stir in her mind – everything about the children is unseasonable, as if they have emerged from her own past in their serge shorts, ragged jerseys, and worn-out oddments of footwear. They are the bad boys in charity clothes she remembers from school. They are covered with the same cuts and scratches and weals and spots. They have the same bony knees, too big for the thin legs, and the same fleshless faces. Their foreheads ripple into parallel lines as careworn as her own, and as familiar.

Suddenly there is an outcry from the smallest boy who has been acting as lookout behind the swarm.

'There it's again!' he shrieks, pointing across the water.

The boys scatter and leap up on the railings, cheering. The marksman takes up position, pulling out the catapult. The ducks are keeping a wide berth. The shout goes up: 'Get it! Get it!' and a battery of pointing fingers follows the course of some hidden enemy.

The stout lady comes to life and makes a try for the catapult, but she is heavy and slow. There is a scuffle during which the weapon changes hands half a dozen times. In a few seconds the boy is ten paces away, the catapult back in his hands. He fires off a pebble which plops harmlessly into the water by the near shore.

Groaning and catcalling, the lads shade their eyes and peer after the quarry, signalling for the next volley.

The stout lady sees her chance and pounces again.

'If that's not shooting birds . . . !' she exclaims, raising the guilty arm to full length. The arm twists in her hand with such energy that she is pulled about. Her mauve hat tilts and her hair loosens. The two brittle bones in the forearm she is clutching are working like pistons under the rough wool, hot from the sun. The catapult waves in the air. She tries unsuccessfully to reach it, and the struggle leaves her gasping for breath.

'It's no' a bird! It's no' a bird, missis!' The boy is in misery. There is no justice, and his prey is escaping.

The lady berates him harshly for telling lies, but her companion has the better view, and sees what the boys are after.

'Look – ' she says. 'It's a water rat, poor thing!'

The rat bustles about in the shadow of some weeds where the roots of the tree snake into the water. The animal frisks this way and that. Then it darts into the water and swims forward for a yard or so, trailing a neat, arrowheaded wake. The sight drives the boys into a frenzy.

'Get it! Get it!' they scream at their marksman who flings himself out of his captor's grasp and looses a shot straight for the creature's head. At the splash, the rat veers towards the island, slides on to a small rock and runs towards a hole under the tree roots. Another pebble skims into the nearby weeds. The rat bellies down into the shadows and is gone.

The disappointment is total. The boys throw themselves from the railings and beat their heads with their fists in a pantomime of grief. They yell invective at the watchers on the benches, at the two elderly ladies, and especially at the marksman.

'*They* pit me aff!' he shouts back. 'It's no' ma fault!'

The old lady is getting more and more agitated. 'A poor wee water rat that does nobody any harm!'

The marksman rounds on her. 'Aye it does! Ye know whit it did?'

Again the boys swarm round the ladies who edge nervously together. Then the smallest boy is manhandled to the fore-front. He smells of dry urine. His left foot is grabbed from the ground and pressed up as high as it will go so that the ladies can observe it at close quarters. Its owner, propped on the narrow chest of the tall lad, remains unruffled by the treat-ment. He fixes on the stout lady a gaze lucent with martyr-dom.

The ladies would rather not come too close to the skinny leg that rears up at them, but the marksman urges them for-ward.

'See ma wee brother's toe!'

It can't be missed. It protrudes unmistakably from the frayed black sandshoe, only a few inches from their eyes. Under the black-edged toenail there is a fiery triangular wound.

'It bit him!' cries the boy, his voice vibrating through their heads. He is triumphant – he is vindicated. There can be no doubting the material evidence.

The ladies grit their teeth as if in pain as they stare at the wounded toe swaying near their faces.

'It's for it!' the boy exclaims tersely. 'It's no' gettin' away wi' that – bitin' ma wee brother's toe! We're only gettin' it back.'

The cry is taken up by the others. 'It's for it!' The damaged leg is dropped to the ground where it rejoins the scuffling, wrestling throng. The leg has served its purpose. Vengeance is the imperative once more.

The stout lady still has the ringleader by the arm. 'Listen, son, what was he up to when it bit him, eh?'

'He wuz asleep – it wuz inty his bed this mornin'! It's no' gettin' away wi' bitin' ma wee brother! Is it there?' he yells over his shoulder to the martyr, who is acting as lookout on the railings again.

'No' yet!' the reply sings back.

The diversion succeeds. The captive tugs himself free. All attention shifts back to the island. Once more the railing is lined with a fanatical horde shrieking ferociously across the water at the island. A plane passes overhead towing two streamers of cloud across the blue sky, but its jets cannot drown the high-pitched frenzy below.

The two ladies stand by helplessly, the younger looking round as if she would like to summon help. The few passers-by pay no attention. The spectators on the benches look back with vague, uncommitted stares. The sun glitters on the road and fills the hot, still air with sparkling specks of dust, and the pigeons high on the tree indulge in soft demonstrations of affection. The seagull overtops them all, white and remote on one thin leg.

The stout lady brings her mauve hat close beside her friend's black one. 'I think we should get the police.'

The old lady is tired and out of sorts, and her eyes are moist. 'Don't be daft,' she says with a spurt of venom, and adds under her breath, 'Wee devils. Poor wee devils.'

There is a sudden uproar that outdoes anything that has gone before, and every wing is set in flight.

'The Parkie! The Parkie!'

Boys and birds scatter to the four winds, and in the strange quiet that follows, a Park Ranger wanders into view, fanning his mild sunburned face with his official hat.

THE EQUAL OF HER SMILE

Richard Fletcher

After a drive of more than two hundred miles, Mr Wooler became lost in the streets that teeter uphill behind Dunoon's smart esplanades. Taking directions from a vague old man outside a public house, he rounded one last corner and reached his goal, a drab Edwardian terrace, at half past three.

As he stopped the car he wondered if his wife was watching. She would not recognize the car – Mr Wooler changed his car every five years – but she would, he supposed, recognize him. It was hot and the journey had left him with a headache; not severe, for Mr Wooler permitted neither extremes nor sunglasses.

He turned off the engine and sat for a moment of contemplation and rehearsal.

'I'm sorry to surprise you like this, Alice.'

But would she let him in? Or would she crouch behind her letter box, her amber eyes glinting with abuse, snarling at him like a leopard? Surely in seven years she must have mellowed? Surely?

Mr Wooler sighed and got out of his car. He locked the door. He tugged the handle. He tested the other doors the same way. He did not forget the boot. Satisfied, he dropped his keys into the pocket he used for key carrying.

He told himself that he was calm and in such a frame of mind that reason would prevail, although his solicitor had long ago advised him to wade in there and thump her. But Mr Wooler was the sort of man who pressed his fingertips earnestly together; who did not smoke; who liked dogs but did not have one. All his shirts were the same colour and he had not been brought up to thump the other sex.

'I really can't see that striking her would achieve anything, in the circumstances,' Mr Wooler had said. Yet his loins had stirred; not earnestly, but they had stirred.

'Humph!' his solicitor had replied, closing one creased and blood-smirched eye and peering at Mr Wooler, the better to assess his chances.

Standing now, not without a sense of trespass, on his wife's stretch of pavement, Mr Wooler thought – No! No fisticuffs. Rational, adult discussion, that's the thing.

He scrutinized his wife's front door as though he expected hatches to slide open revealing primed cannon.

He tapped with a knocker shaped like a bulldog's head.

'Rational,' he repeated.

The houses had no front gardens. Gratings in the pavement sliced up the daylight for basements where people actually lived. The basement of Mr Wooler's house had no windows and no light got in and it was cluttered with fragments of flower pots. His wife had smashed the flower pots before she walked out. She had ripped the pendulum out of his grandfather clock. She had cut his lovely purple cummerbund into shreds strewn round their bedroom and along the landing. His aspirins, shaving tackle and cough lozenges had been swept into the bath as by one blow. She had taken nothing but her clothes, some jewellery cashable only in nostalgia, and the child, then two years old.

'Adult,' murmured Mr Wooler, tapping again.

His wife's voice called from the upper part of the house.

'It's open. Come up.'

He knocked louder, resenting her neighbourliness. The response was a clattering of utensils and her footsteps coming down carpetless stairs.

Mr Wooler's heart began to hammer. Suppose she ran him off her patch with grape-shot invective? The inside of Mr Wooler's mouth went dry.

'Who is it?'

He made no answer. Let her open up. Let her find out.

The door between them swung wide.

There was flour on the frames of her glasses and on her hands. Her nose was floury, as was her hair, which had been short but now swung to her shoulders. She was wearing something blue.

'What's this?' she said, with no hint of surprise. 'The end of the seven lean years?'

'Hallo, Alice,' he said.

'Or the start of a plague of boils?'

Before he could speak she went on, 'I was baking. For Eva's school party.'

'School? Why, of course.'

'She's nine now.'

'Nine,' he marvelled. 'Of course.'

He was going to say 'Time flies' but checked himself.

She is still magnificent, he thought. Sleek, like a race-horse.

'What do you want?' the racehorse asked, nostrils flaring. 'Why don't you bugger off?'

'I hoped we might talk.'

'To what purpose?'

'I'm sorry I didn't let you know.'

'In case I happened to be out?'

He said nothing.

'Well?' she asked.

'Must we talk on the doorstep?'

The mocking smile he had endured so often spread over her face. She dropped her voice to a stage whisper.

'How do you know . . . I haven't got a fella . . . ?' She jerked her thumb in the direction of the stairs. 'Up there?'

He wanted to say 'You would not, because of the child.' Curiously, he felt certain of this.

163

'No doubt your behaviour has been as proper as mine,' he said, and regretted it.

'Have you trundled your insufferable smugness all the way from Yorkshire in one day? You always were one for marathon drives, weren't you?'

There was a short silence. Then she seemed to come to a decision.

'I suppose I'll have to make you tea. Come on then.'

He followed her up the stairs on pine treads uncarpeted by design, not by poverty. She climbed as an athlete would, on her toes.

'Do you have the whole house?' he asked.

Her calf muscles tensed and softened.

'None of your business.'

He kept his silence, thinking that she had not changed, wondering if he were to touch the skin behind her knee, would she turn and kick him in the teeth.

She showed him into a room that overlooked the street, a living-room separated by an archway from a kitchen done in dark wood and brassware. Her baking covered a table placed in the arch. The room smelled of fresh cooked pastry and gingerbread and was warm and sunny. He felt the contentment in it with a pang. On one wall were pinned childish drawings with the beginnings of style. There were framed pen and ink drawings too; of a grinning schoolgirl; a group of three magpies; and a self portrait, kneeling naked, arms outflung, hair streaming.

'You still draw?'

'And teach. But I had to change my technique.'

'Oh? Why?'

'Don't bother me with questions. Sit! Go on . . . sit down!' She waved him to a chair.

'Why have you come?'

'What are you baking?' he said.

'Oh, that's marvellous. Stanley, you're a knock-out.'

'I realize this must seem strange . . . ah, popping in on you after seven years . . .'

'Tea or coffee?'

'Tea. Thank you.'

'Strange? But you are strange, Stanley. You're as strange as a three pound note. What am I supposed to think, after seven years?'

As she filled the kettle he noticed that she held it awkwardly.

'If you don't mind, I'll carry on with my pastry while you do your talking. Do you still do the same talky job with all those talky people? The rooms you used to fill with your talk.'

She flipped a sheet of pastry over and over, dusting it with flour from a shaker held awkwardly also.

'Yes,' he said. 'Still the same place. But I've had a couple of promotions.'

'Now you can talk down to everybody, eh?'

I should have expected that, he thought, and made no more of his success. He raised a mild hand.

'Yes. Yes. I do . . . do probably talk too much. Always did.'

She picked up her rolling pin. He noticed the fingers of her right hand seemed curled as if by cramp.

'Have you hurt your hand?' he asked.

'I put it through a glass door . . . in my first school after . . . after I came here. All the tendons were cut. For a time it looked like amputation. The fingers will move just enough to hold my brushes. It was my own fault.'

'I didn't know.'

'Of course not.'

It could have been her face, he thought.

'Serves me right.'

'What?' he asked.

'That's what you're thinking, isn't it?'

'What?'

'Pay the bitch out for leaving you.'

'Don't be ridiculous. You misjudge me.'

The kettle boiled.

'Can I help?' he asked.

'It did not disable me.' She sounded angry.

'No. I am truly sorry. Please believe that.'

'I scarcely notice now. I don't need pity.'

'Eva would be . . .'

'Just out of nappies. I had good help. I managed.'

She made tea, arranging cups and saucers on a tray with great speed, the crippled hand nudging and steadying, while he imagined the cascade of glass and blood. Had it cracked her calm? He could not see Alice screaming for help. She would have walked to the Head's study, her good hand clamped on the pumping wound saying 'I've had an accident. Call an ambulance, Headmaster.' Perhaps then she might have fainted, but tidily, using a chair, not in an undignified heap on the Head's floor. And the school would have sent the brasher girls with flowers to the hospital and welcomed her return by cheering and clapping when she took the platform, slinged and smiling, at morning assembly.

'You have far too sweet a tooth, I remember,' she said.

'Yes.' He laughed.

'It shows.'

He did not know what to say. She placed his cup on the table where she was working.

'There you are,' she said, not looking at him. 'Help yourself.'

She picked up her rolling pin again. Carrying the cup, he crossed to the window. Two small girls were passing, sharing an ice cream, lick by lick.

'Where is Eva?' he said.

'At Brownie Camp. For the weekend. What a pity you won't see her.'

'Brownies,' he said. 'Goodness.'

Her rolling pin thumped.

'Stanley, what on earth do you want?'

He turned from the window and did not know what to say, and sat down again.

'Do you even know yourself?' she asked.

He considered this. She turned her pastry this way and that with her left hand while the other gripped the pin. He did not know, absolutely, why he had come.

'Do you want me to come back to you?'

She looked directly at him with such frank eyes that he was startled. He could not answer, for she would make 'No' an insult and turn 'Yes' to scorn. He considered turning the question back on her. 'Do you want to come back, Alice?' But this would only invite a rebuke.

'Does she like the Brownies?' he said.

She folded the pastry on itself and on an imprecation.

'Do you love me, Stanley? Have you been pining away all these years? No . . . you didn't get a pot like that from pining, did you. I bet . . . I bet you have girls up in the bedroom, don't you, Stanley. Wriggly eighteen-year-olds who tell you you're marvellous and your wife was a bitch and rub oil in your back.' Her smile showed her fine square teeth.

'No . . . I know!' she cried. 'You've got a seven year itch. Hee! Hee! Oil's just the thing for that, Stanley.'

'Alice!'

No one had ever rubbed oil into his back.

'Alice!' she mocked, her head on one side.

He pressed his knees together. His cup rattled in the saucer. He would not be baited. He would not lose his temper.

'There are things we should discuss. Should have discussed a long time ago.'

'But it took you such a long time to get here, Stanley.'

'I . . .'

'You were scared, Stanley.' She rolled the pastry vigorously.

He could not answer. He knew she was right. He blundered on.

'Financial arrangements. Eva's school . . . I can pay for Eva to go to school . . .'

'I keep myself. Eva can always go to my school. Good heavens, Stanley, I wouldn't leave you flat and then take subsidies for my desertion.'

'You admit desertion?'

'Oh yes! Of course. No argument.'

'You may wish to marry again?'

'Do you?' she asked.

Before he could answer she went on.

'Not me. Once was enough. Let's stay the way we are, with our love a little flower pressed in our prayer books . . . a comfort for our declining years.'

'I do wish you'd be serious.'

'But you're not.'

'Of course . . . or I wouldn't be here.'

'Rubbish!'

She put down her rolling pin.

'Stanley, you meandered up here on the spur of the moment. You know you did. Whatever possessed you? Was it because of the nice day? Had you a plan? You had no plan. What do you want?'

'I hoped I'd learn what you want.'

'Christ!'

'Alice . . .'

'I have what I want,' she said. 'All I want. My work. My friends. Eva.'

'My child.'

'I settled my conscience years ago.'

'Is Eva . . . ?' he began.

'Damaged by it. No.'

'Doesn't she ask about me?'

'Do you wonder about her?'

'Of course I do,' he said, seeing from the way her face closed that the conversation had come to a cul-de-sac. Their brief marriage had been nothing but cul-de-sacs.

He sipped his tea.

'Why did you chose Dunoon?'

She pressed tart cases from the pastry with a crinkly cutter. Her brow furrowed; theatrically, he thought.

'It's . . .' She stopped. 'Perhaps because it's like me.'

'Like you?'

'Yes.'

'Dunoon?'

'Yes. A raddled old tart behind a lot of fancy make-up.'

'That's silly. A veiled search for compliments.'

She used the wrist of her damaged hand to hold a jar against her waist while she spooned jam.

'They'd go to my head, I suppose?'

'What I was never sure of,' he began, choosing his words cautiously for the minefields ahead, 'is . . .'

The click of her spoon in the jar stopped.

'Is why I left you?'

'Well . . .'

'Do you want a divorce? Is that it? I wouldn't stop you.'

'Couldn't,' he said with emphasis.

'Of course I could. I said I wouldn't. Stop being silly.'

'But you couldn't,' he insisted. 'Not after all this time. The reformed divorce law allows me to . . .'

'Stanley! I don't want a windy explanation of the niceties of the divorce laws. I said I could stop you and I meant it. It would take me about five minutes, I should think.'

The radiance of her smile should have warned him, but his irritation rose like a dog's hackles.

'You may overvalue your talents in many directions, Alice, but even you cannot re-write the divorce laws unilaterally to

suit your whims. Today, tomorrow, I could raise an action on
the grounds of the irretrievable breakdown of our mar-
iage . . .'

'Of our fiddlesticks! Anyway, who decides it's broken
down? It's a perfectly serviceable old marriage. It's you that's
broken down, Stanley. Now drink up your tea and stop
sounding so puffy.'

'But what do you mean? Just how would you stop me?
What would you do? The law is the law.'

'But I'm an outlaw, Stanley. Didn't you know that? Oh
dear.'

With an exaggerated sigh, she resumed her spooning while
he struggled with a rising frustration. She had not mellowed.
She had in no way changed. She still refused to concede that
words had precise meanings which must be taken note of if
orderly relationships were to be established. He also knew
the pointlessness of carrying on the argument.

'What did you tell your colleagues?'

Her smile was back and the edge of mischief in her voice.

'I wish you wouldn't turn my questions.'

She filled the last of her pastry cases and put the trayful into
the top oven of her cooker.

'Did you tell them I was taking a long holiday?'

'I told them what was true, of course.'

'True? I thought that perhaps you'd tell them you'd had
me committed.' She laughed.

'Don't be preposterous!'

'Imagine it! "Mrs Wooler's in the Bin. Did you know?"
"Poor old Stanley." "Poor long-suffering old chap." "Didn't
we always say she was doo-lally." Oh, Stanley, it would have
been a lovely excuse.'

'Excuse?'

'Yes. You know . . . saved your stuffy old face. Long,
lugubrious old face . . . and it would have fitted the facts.'

'Facts?' He knew well what she meant but wanted her

own admission that she had behaved outrageously. She only laughed and set the oven timer and came round her baking table to sit in a rocking chair. She rested her head and rocked with her body, keeping her feet on the floor. She wore wooden exercise clogs with canvas tops. Her feet were bare and brown. Her crabbed right hand gripped the chair arm, its wreckage accenting her beauty like a squint in a lovely face. She rocked and her laughter came in bubbles and he knew she was remembering.

He could forgive her the public humiliations; her bizarre forms of unsocial behaviour, culminating in an attempted strip-tease requiring forcible restraint, at a party given by his office manager, a solid fellow used to dependable cooks and secretaries. It was the private ones, hurtful at first and then merely puzzling, that still distressed him.

As if reading his thoughts she said,

'What a way to repay your kindness. I suppose you were kind.'

'I could never work you out,' he said, encouraged.

'Well you know, Stanley . . . Woman . . . ever mysterious.'

'You could never be persuaded to discuss our . . . difficulties.'

Her chair came slowly upright. She looked at him, her eyelids drooping slightly.

'*Our* difficulties. What a cheek!'

'I will accept that in some measure . . . possibly in greater measure than you, I was to blame. But you cannot pretend . . . well, you may pretend, but you do not deceive yourself that you were wholly free from blemish. No, no. I say . . . I will accept blame, though quite what my sins were I have never been sure . . .'

'Sins?'

'Well . . . not sins perhaps . . . but there must have been some tangible reasons for your leaving . . .'

'Did I need reasons? Outlaws need no reasons.'

'Really, Alice! This is preposterous. I am trying to help us. I came down here, at some inconvenience to my schedule, I might add . . . to see if we couldn't work out something sensible.'

'Oh I see! That's what you came for. To work out something sensible. I'm sorry that was inconvenient for you.'

'Alice!' He made his voice a little sterner.

She sat upright.

'Yes? Yes, Stanley?' She spoke quickly, clipping the words. He pressed on.

'I hoped we might be able to discuss . . . sensibly . . . why you left. If we could only talk things over . . . I might be able . . .'

'Yes, Stanley? Yes? Yes? What?'

He spread his hands. He pressed his fingertips earnestly together.

'Well, I might be able to work something . . . more sensible out.'

'You said that.'

'What?'

'Something sensible. To be able to work it out or something.'

'We could never talk,' he blurted. 'I could never . . . what's the expression . . . get through to you.'

'No.' She gazed at the ceiling. 'I'm your femme fatale, Stanley.'

'I still think . . .'

'What?' she said, but her tone had changed and become wintry.

'You should tell me . . . why you left. I have a right to know!'

'Why I left? You have a right? You have a left – right – left. Do you always march about in suits, Stanley? Do you never knock about in an old sweater and trousers with rips in the knees?'

She stood up.

'What would talking settle? What do you want to know *for*? To be happier in your misery? Discussions like this make my flesh creep.'

'Alice. For once. Be reasonable.'

'Will you excuse me a moment? Help yourself to more tea. I've set the oven timer for my pastry. I should be back ... but if it buzzes, would you ...?'

She handed him a yellow oven glove with the words 'Tomorrow We Eat in Town' printed on it. He accepted it absently.

'Leave the oven on though. I've another batch to do.'

Her smile sparkled. 'Won't be long.'

'Where are you going?' he asked.

'Goodness, Stanley, you never ask a lady where she's going.'

As she left the room he half rose from his seat.

'You were always such a gentleman,' she said as the door closed after her. Then she poked her head back into the room.

'All right,' she said. 'I will tell you.'

'What?' Neither standing nor sitting, he gazed at her.

'Why I left you. Because calling you Stan was always quite out of the question. And do close your mouth.'

She was gone before he could ask her what she meant. But she did not leave the house and in a moment he heard her singing, a few ironic bars from 'Butterfly', her voice as high and clear as he remembered it.

He sighed. The trouble had begun the very day of their wedding, with summer rain gusting against the church windows while he proudly escorted his bride, unprepared for the furies ahead. Even as they came down the aisle she whispered a startling paraphrase of Hamlet's great soliloquy, relevant perhaps to wedding days but distasteful to a virgin bridegroom and certainly intemperate in the House of God. On their honeymoon, which she afterwards referred to as the syrupmoon, she had flirted outrageously with barmen, hotel undermanagers and the embarrassed husbands of equally recent brides.

And now? What had calling him Stan got to do with it? No one called him Stan, not even his peers at the office. Stanley, he had always thought, was a name with a dignity befitting his recently won managership. But let her call him Stan if she wished. Why was it out of the question and what possible difference could it make?

Where was he to go from here? If he were to persuade her to return, what was he letting himself in for? Where did Eva fit into his plans, if indeed he had any? He could imagine Eva wrinkling her nose when Alice said 'This is your father.'

The buzzer on the oven drilled into these gloomy thoughts. Let them burn, he thought, but he was at the oven and reaching into it for the baking tray, his hand warm in the mitten, when the door flew open and Alice rushed into the room, her clogs clattering on the wooden floor. The buzzer was still going. He had not been able to see, among the array of knobs and switches, how to turn it off.

'I'll get it,' Alice said. 'Oh . . . you've taken them out.'

He turned with the tray in his hands.

'Alice!'

She had only her clogs on and a pair of brief pale blue knickers with a darker blue embroidered pattern.

'Put them on the table,' she said.

She took the tray from him as he averted his eyes.

'Really, Alice!'

She sniffed deeply.

'Ummmmm . . . lovely. Look at them, Stanley. Aren't they gorgeous? Would you like one while they're still warm?'

She stood close to him in the space between the table and her sink and cooker. Her perfume reached him, fresh and heathery, with the smell of pastry and hot jam. He felt trapped by her nudity in the narrow space. It would be impossible to pass her without some sort of contact.

'Alice. For Heaven's sake, go and dress.' He heard his voice squeaking. He stared resolutely out of the kitchen window.

'I heard the buzzer going on and on,' she said. 'I thought perhaps you'd wandered off somewhere. My pastry might have spoiled.'

'Maybe. But I wish you'd get dressed. This is typical of your old exhibitionism. Don't imagine I don't realize why you're behaving like this.'

'But I'm in my own home, Stanley,' she said demurely. 'With my own husband . . . bent only on rescuing my pastry. Don't be an old fuddy-duddy.'

He still looked out of the window. In the backyard of the house next door, three cats stood as though frozen, their tails bristling. They seemed, in their wariness, to be yawning at each other.

He swallowed. Behind him, he heard Alice weighing out flour.

'Why change your frock in the middle of baking? This is just an attempt to discomfit me. It is adolescent.'

'Adolescent? Really? When I was that age I had to be bribed out of my clothes. Fags or motor-bike rides did the trick. Are today's pubescents more forthcoming?'

'Surely you have a housecoat or something?' he said, turning.

'Eeek!' she said. 'A male person with his eyes upon me!'

She crossed her forearms in front of her. Her injured hand rested, a pink claw, against her shoulder.

'Let me past,' he demanded, looking over her head. 'I won't be subjected to this.'

He brushed by her.

'You'll never grow up,' he said. 'Your outlook on life is a child's. A distortion. You should think of Eva, how she will be affected by it. And show some responsibility.'

'But Eva isn't here. Anyway, she often sees me in the buff.'

'I meant in general. You know perfectly well what I meant.'

'Now . . . where did I put my lard?'

He could follow what she did by the sound of weights banging on the scale pan and ingredients tipping into the mixing bowl.

'I can't manage properly with my fingers any more,' she said.

He sucked in his breath and came to a decision.

'I shall leave,' he said.

She switched on an electric mixer.

'I don't like these things,' she shouted over the machine's rising whine, 'but my hand . . . you know.'

'That is, unless you've anything to say.'

'What?' she shouted.

'I said, I shall leave unless you've anything to say,' he shouted back.

'No! You've said it all!'

He stood uncertainly for a moment.

'Well then . . .' He turned to the door, still not looking at her.

'Bye!' she called, brightly.

He left the room.

'Damn,' he said to himself. 'Damn. Damn. Damn.'

When he was half-way down the stairs the mixer stopped. He hesitated but went on down. Had she weakened? Did she want him not to go? Three steps from the bottom something struck him hard just below the shoulder and a second later, her other clog clattered past him and thudded against the front door.

'Good riddance!' she yelled.

He did not look back and as the door closed he heard her shouting something about him being as puny as a shirt button.

Typical, he thought. Yes, going was the right thing to do. She was clearly beyond the reach of reason. Coming to Dunoon had been a mistake after all. He would instruct his solicitor. He felt in his pocket for his car keys.

Upstairs, Alice stood looking at the closed door. Her clogs lay close to each other at the stair foot, in a patch of sunshine. She heard his car start up and drive away and the street grow very quiet. She turned to her reflection in a mirror on the landing. She began to cry. For a few moments she cried bitterly.

'He had such fine shoulders,' she sobbed. 'Lion's shoulders.'

If only he would refuse to stand for her nonsense. If only he would stop nit-picking his way through it and silence her with some decisive act or even with laughter.

She blinked away her tears at last, her lower lip trembling, until her crying had ceased to sting and only her sorrow remained. Suddenly she felt cold. Her hand ached. She had waited so long.

'Pout!' she commanded. Her reflection pouted.

'That's better!'

The line of her lip slowly lengthened as her smile gathered and her white teeth glistened. She winked at herself. Being after all more than a match for Mr Wooler, it was a comfort to know that she was at least the equal of her smile.

She went to the bedroom and made up her eyes and slipped her blue dress on again, and from there to the kitchen, to face her baking and the years that waited for her.

LEAVE IT TO THE RIVER

P. M. Hubbard

They say the river takes a life a year, but they say that, or
something like it, about half the rivers in these islands. The
experts will have it that it all goes back to the days when rivers
were gods and, like all gods, potentially destructive unless
propitiated by sacrifice. I doubt many people think the river a
god now, but a lot still believe in the annual quota, or perhaps
the river itself has just got into the habit of it, even though its
power for mischief, like that of other gods and natural phen-
omena, has been much eroded by man's increasing ability to
look after himself. I only know that last summer, when a
young man employed on the bridge works fell in and was
never seen again, there were those who expressed relief that
the river had taken its life for the year during the summer
(and an Englander at that), and so made life safer for the locals
who had anything to do with it during its more dangerous
season.

Not being a fisherman or a riparian owner, I myself do not
have much to do with the river at any time, but I sail my boat
on the salt water of the bay it runs into, and where the river
ends and the sea begins is a matter you could greatly exercise
your mind on, if you are a man given to mental exercise. A
big flood tide when the river itself is in spate can pile the
water up till it roars under the soffits of the bridge, and a big
ebb can leave the land-water a wee ribbon in the vast ex-
panse of mud which is then the surface of the bay. The fact remains that whatever the river brings down the sea takes and
deals with in its own fashion, and if, as it might be once a year
or so, the river brings down a human body, it is likely the sea

that will do the burying of it, unless someone sees it and fishes
it out before it gets that far. It is the sea that will have taken
the young Englander from the bridge works. Maybe it took
him back to the English coast, so that he came north by land
and went south by water, as a lot of people used to do before
the ports on the bay silted up, and the regular passenger
services to Cumberland stopped operating.

I fancy I know of one life the river was reckoned to have
taken but did not take and another it might, in a sense, have
taken but would not. But that's some years back. Nichol Mair
is well dead now, and his Jeannie safely married and away to
another part of the country, and in any case those are not their
real names. At the time I kept quiet about it and left it to the
river, or maybe it was the sea, to decide the thing, but there
seems no harm in speaking of it now. Not, I assure you, to
unburden my conscience. I do not find, at my time of life,
that my conscience is much given to burdens, and in any case
I never had an ill conscience where Nichol Mair was concerned. But I tell it for the interest of the thing, and because
the young Englander from the bridge works, disappearing the
way he did, has put me in mind of it.

Nichol Mair was a forester, and had been all his working
life. By the time I knew him he was employed, like nearly
all of them, by the Commission, but he had started in private
service in the days when the big estates had their own
foresters, and when the foresters still felled with the axe
instead of the whining chain-saws that nowadays can make a
stretch of hill forest as peaceful in season as a go-kart track on
a Saturday afternoon. He was not a tall man – they do not
run much to height in these parts – but very broad and strong
and red-faced, and he still had his axe and looked after it as a
concert violinist looks after his fiddle. If there was axe-work
to be done (and there still is at times, even now), it was Nichol
they put on to it, and he had no aversion to showing the boys
what he could do with his axe, either in the way of business or

sometimes, when he had taken a dram or two, just for the hell of it or for a bet, if he could find anyone rash enough to bet against him. I had heard many stories of his accomplishments in that direction, but never saw any of them for myself, not being around at the right times and places.

One other thing Nichol had which he looked after even more carefully than his axe, and took no bets on drunk or sober, and that was his daughter Jeannie, Jeannie's mother having died a while before I first knew him. Whether Jeannie's mother was ever precisely married to Nichol was a thing you heard different views of, but the technicalities of marriage are not much thought of in these parts, and either way she had lived with him most of his working life, and had brought up Jeannie as strictly as if she had been a daughter of the manse or the progeny of a pedigree saddleback Galloway. By the time I am speaking of there were those who said that Jeannie was better able to look after Nichol than he was to look after her, though in the nature of things less forward at it. She was a slender slip of a girl, pale-skinned and dark-haired and a bit slant-eyed, of a type you see in a while round here, very striking in contrast to the four-square twopence-coloured women who make up the most of our female population, and clearly coming from a different stock, which for all I know may be new-come Irish or prehistoric Pictish, but is certainly, as I say, very distinctive. The mother I never saw, but she must have been very much of that sort herself to have produced Jeannie to Nichol Mair's fathering.

Whether or not Jeannie was capable of looking after Nichol, I would say (and that was the general view) that she was well capable of looking after herself. With those looks and the manner of acting and speaking her mother had somehow given her, the men were round her like wasps round a beer-spill before she was well sixteen, and she handled them with the effortless composure of an old dog with the daft hoggets, even men much older than herself. Not that she was stand-

offish, she was all for a good time, was Jeannie Mair, and there
were those who said she was not above lending herself whiles
to a man she fancied, but never for keeps. That may have been
the plain ill-nature of other girls, or their mothers, or maybe
the men she didn't fancy well enough. There is always plenty
of ill-nature about a girl like Jeannie whatever she does, and I
would not say we are more given to charitable talking than
most other rural communities. Certainly she was never in any
sort of trouble, but then a girl with her head screwed on as
tight as Jeannie's doesn't get into trouble these days. Presently
she would pick a man she reckoned up to her and settle down,
and there was a good deal of speculation who it would be, with
the odds constantly changing.

Whether Nichol worried about his Jeannie I cannot say. He
was proud of her to the point of daftness and gave her whatever he could she wanted, and as she had her own money from
working in the one smart dress shop, she was always turned
out in a style most of the other girls couldn't hope to match,
not with the figures they had and the taste for bright colours
which is so marked in these parts. (Jeannie herself wore only
simple, plain-coloured clothes, which lit her up like a black
candle.) From what came of it, Nichol must have watched
over her in a quiet way, but to all outward appearances he let
her have her head in most things, if indeed he had even been
capable of controlling her, which I would say was doubtful.

At the time I am speaking of (which would be the Septem-
ber of three or four years back) the most favoured claimant
to Jeannie's hand was young Macalister, who worked in the
bank, no less. Favoured, I mean, by general public estim-
ation. In what way Jeannie favoured him there is no saying,
but my guess would be that, whatever she did elsewhere,
Jeannie would have no favours, in the more particular sense,
to bestow on her chosen man until she had got him publicly
signed up in the church with full honours and the white
bridal gown of only now negotiable virginity. Young Mac-

alister (Jimmie, he called himself, and a proper Jimmie he looked, too, to my way of thinking) was a posting to our branch from farther east. He was as smooth and smart in his way as Jeannie was in hers, but without the underlying wildness. He wore well-cut dark suits and equally well-cut sandy whiskers, and all but fluttered his eyelashes at you as he cashed your cheque and counted out your dirty notes with his pretty, chopped hands. But he would be a bank manager some day, and that was a far call from a forester's cottage, and he had the added qualification that Jeannie would plainly run rings round him as soon as he had got his ring on her. All that being so, Nichol no doubt favoured him as a son-in-law, whatever he thought of him as a man, and that would have been worth hearing, too, if he could have been brought to say it, only he never said anything, even in his cups, which had any bearing on Jeannie. So at that stage it looked all set for a happy ending, for Nichol and Jeannie at least, and presumably also for Jimmie Macalister if he would be content to take her for richer rather than poorer, but any road for better or worse.

It was then that the villain appeared in the shape of Jack Robson. He was a posting to our parts, too, but from the south, not the east, and he was posted, not to the bank, but to the local division of the Forestry Commission itself; so that if he was not Nichol's actual boss, he had at least a say in what Nichol would be doing and where he would be sent to do it. When I said Jack Robson was the villain, I used the word in its dramatic or literary sense, but that wasn't the only sort of villain he was, not by a long cast. I do not reckon to be censorious with my fellow creatures now, any more than I do with myself, and I can keep on terms with the generality of people hereabouts, even if there are some I would not buy a pound of potatoes from unless I saw it weighed and many more I would not go drinking with in any circumstances at all. But Jack Robson was a bad man if ever I saw one, and smooth with it in an English way, though he came from no farther south than Carlisle, but with all his smoothness mean and hard and nasty. He was as good-looking as Jimmie Macalister, though dark and sharp-faced instead of soft-faced and sandy, but in other ways he could not well be more different in style. He was what they used to call flash, and for all he spent much of his time in the office or riding round in a Land-Rover, he got himself up like a second-feature lumber-jack, with a zipper jacket of black and white woollen check and lace-up boots to the top of his calves. And to my way of judging at least, and it soon appeared not only to mine, he had as much sex-appeal in his little finger as Jimmie had in his whole body from his sandy crown to the soles of his bright black step-in shoes. Nor had this gift of nature gone un-noticed by Jack himself, and as soon as he got settled in, he was off after the local women with the single-minded en-thusiasm of a fox in the hen-run.

I say the local women, meaning in general, and to start with that was the way of it, and if half what I heard was true, he had grassed a fair catch of them in his first season among us, including some of the young grilse that hadn't reckoned to be taken by anyone for a while yet, or not until Jack came after them. And if Jack wasn't the only one for the sport in these parts, he was quicker and harder at it than most, and he talked more about it afterwards. But after a bit he seemingly got tired of this promiscuous ravaging and settled to a serious siege operation, and the target he picked on was inevitably Jeannie Mair. I say inevitably, because for a man who thought he could take his pick, she was the obvious one to pick on, and the fact that she was a girl who made her own decisions and would not be rushed into them was strong drink to a man of his nature. I suppose with an administrative position in what may be called a career service he might be considered as good a matrimonial prospect in economic terms as Jimmie Macalister, but the girl who would consider Jack as a husband in any other terms would need her head examining, which Jeannie certainly did not. As I saw it, the danger was not that Jeannie might marry him, even if he asked her, which was unlikely, but that he might queer her pitch with Jimmie Macalister. But they were two independent creatures and must settle it between them, and the rest of us stood back and held our breath if not in all cases our tongues. What Nichol thought no one knew, because, as always when it was anything to do with Jeannie, he never said, but it is not to be supposed that he was happy about it.

That was the position of things in mid-September, when the big tides came in, and with the rain we had had on the hills northward the river was in full spate, and at high water the fields downstream were covered, and in the town itself the water was up to the arches of the bridge and licking at the walls of the gardens that went down to the bank. As it happened, one of these gardens was Nichol's. He had a cottage near the end of the town, which is at best only the one street running parallel with the river, with the bridge taking off in the middle and the houses on one side with their backs to the higher ground and those on the other with their backs, at some remove, to the river. Nobody knows rightly what happened that night except Nichol himself, and he's dead now, though for reasons of my own I have my own idea of it, and I cannot altogether avoid the speculation that Jeannie may have hers too. But officially Jeannie was not there, though admittedly thereby, and I had no reason to say anything then, nor would I if I had, so the only account of the matter was the one Nichol gave to Sergeant Menzies when he knocked him up at the police station a bit after midnight.

Nichol's story was that he had come home at eleven, when the drinking officially stops, and found Jack Robson at one of the back windows of the cottage, the window being in fact that of Jeannie's bedroom and Jeannie herself doucely asleep inside. They had had what he called a bit of an altercation,

which seemed natural enough in the circumstances, and Jack
had run off down the garden with Nichol after him, and got
over the garden wall, maybe thinking to escape along the
bank, but instead had slipped on the wet grass and gone into
the water. It had been high water a bit after ten, and by then
the river was going down as fast as a mill-race only wider and
deeper out of all proportion, and what with that and the darkness he had lost sight of Jack at once. For all he knew, he told
the sergeant, Jack might have got out of the water somewhere
downstream, but on the face of it the chances were on the
slender side, so he had thought it right to report the accident
in the proper quarter.

Now Sergeant Menzies may well have had his doubts about
the precise nature of the altercation Nichol had had with Jack,
and it is to be said that although Jack was no doubt agile and
strong for his weight, he would have had no chance at all with
Nichol if the two of them had actually come to grips, which
Nichol swore they had not. But there was likely to be no
evidence but that of Nichol himself unless Jack turned up,
dead or alive. If he turned up alive, there would be his direct
evidence to set against Nichol's, and if dead, there would
maybe be some circumstantial evidence indicating the manner
of his death, but for the moment there was only Nichol's
account of the matter, and with that the sergeant had to be
content.

To nobody's surprise, with the river as it was, Jack did not
turn up in either condition, and by the next day it was the
general view that the river had taken its man, and might well
have made a worse choice of it, and if there were maybe one
or two among the women who did not altogether agree on the
second count, they kept their disagreement to themselves.
The police as in duty bound searched the banks downstream
when the water allowed them, but found nothing, and that
was no great surprise either, the river being in general un-
willing to give up its dead once it had them in its keeping, so

Jack Robson was presumed dead by drowning, and there the matter rested.

There were two things that happened after that. The first was that a couple of days later a boy was drowned a mile upstream. There had been the three boys fishing where and when they should not have been, and one of them had gone in, and the other two had tried unsuccessfully to get at him from the bank, but had, maybe unheroically but very, very wisely, not tried going in after him. But the river was down a bit by then, and it had been daylight, and they had raised the alarm at once, and the body had been recovered, and a very sad case it was, but boys will be boys, and accidents will happen. Now I would not have it thought that I am a prey to vulgar superstition, but I allow it struck me as unreasonable that the river, with its well-known propensities, should have taken two lives in less than two days, and I had no doubt there were others remarked on it too, but with the tragedy hanging over us, no one was likely to remark on it publicly.

The second thing that happened was that on the day after the boy's death I bumped into Jack Robson myself. I mean bumped into him literally, or rather my boat did. It was time I was getting the boat ashore for the winter, but that day there was sunshine after the rain and a fair wind, and I took her for a last sail on the midday flood and ran down towards the mouth of the bay, and it was there, as I say, that I bumped into Jack Robson. I felt the bump before ever I saw him, but as soon as I did see him, I came up into the wind and stood by to get a better look at him. There was no doubt it was Jack, from the check jacket and the dangling boots, but for the rest the details were unattractive, and I was not inclined to look at them too closely. I wondered, as you may suppose, what I ought to do, but one thing I knew for certain, and that was that I was not having Jack in my boat, not in the state he was in, even if I could have got him into it, which was in any case doubtful. I thought maybe I could get a line on him, though a good long line it would have to be, and tow him ashore, but it was just at that moment that something, it could be the movement of the boat near him, rolled him over in the water, and I saw the back of his head. The scalp was gone back from the bone, not gone away altogether but seemingly drawn back on both sides of the head, so that the whole top of the skull was bare, and along the skull, in a straight line from front to back, there was a long cut clean through the bone and into where the brain had been, and still to some extent was, inside the head.

I thought that, whatever had made that cut (and many people might have ideas on that, including, not least, Sergeant Menzies if he had got a sight of it), it had not in any possible way been made by the river. So the river had taken Jack's body, but it had not taken his life, which meant at least that the boy's death had not been, as it were, wholly unnecessary or unprofitable, though I would not be putting that view forward to the boy's parents, even if I believed it myself, which, as I say, you must not suppose I do. But the river, or it maybe was the sea, had Jack now, and the question was what it would do with him, always supposing I did nothing myself, which I was already much inclined to do. It could send him out to sea until he sank finally, or it could put him ashore on one of the wee, wild beaches down the side of the headland, where a lot of things, driftwood and such, do come ashore, or it could even drift him into the box of one of the fixed salmon nets, which are for ever catching things other than salmon, though not often, I think, as big as Jack. If it put him ashore, I thought it could be reckoned constructively to be taking Nichol Mair's life, or what was worth of it, for all they do not hang people for murder nowadays.

But the more I thought about it, the more I thought it would not do that. There was the boy's death to be considered, if you were to accept that view of things, and I did not see, any more than I had before, why a second life should be necessary, to the river or anyone else. I sat there and thought about it, with the wind flapping the foresail in the quiet sunshine, and the boat going gently down to leeward away from floating Jack, who in the nature of things was less subject to wind pressures than the boat was. The more I thought about it, and the farther I got from Jack, the more I thought I could leave it to the river, and believed, though I use the expression only metaphorically, that the river was to be trusted in the matter. By that time I could no longer even see Jack, though I could not be all that far from him, and that too put heart into me, because there are not many boats on the bay, especially in mid-September, and those that are are mostly intent on their own business.

So in the end I worked the boat's head round with the rudder, and put her across the wind again and made sail for my mooring, and the next day I got her out of the water and reckoned that, if the thing ever came in question, there would be no one likely even to know, let alone swear, that I had not got her out the day before. And I was in the right, too, because no one ever saw Jack Robson again, and Jeannie married Jimmie Macalister in the spring, and he was posted away east again before any real harm could come of it locally, whatever sort of a life she led him elsewhere. And the next year Nichol himself dropped dead, as decent and quiet as you please, while he was at his axe-work after a more than usually hard night, and then there was nothing more to worry about, especially when the river drowned one of the daft caravanners who come in the summer, and the year after that, as I say, it was the Englander from the bridge works. So that you could say the river, whatever its propensities, for the most part looks after its own, that is, if you are of a mind to entertain such way-out beliefs, which I in general am not.

BIOGRAPHICAL NOTES

CAMPBELL BLACK was born in Glasgow; educated Whitehill School, then University of Sussex. Three novels – *Assassins and Victims*, *The Punctual Rape*, *Death's Head*; presently living in Arizona. Married, three sons. A play *And They Used to Star in Movies* has been presented in Edinburgh, Dublin, London, Chicago.

PETER CHALONER was born of English parents in Glasgow in 1949. Both grandmothers were Irish, the maternal one born in India. Consequently travel fascinated him from an early age. By twenty-three he had travelled on every continent except Australia. He spent 1971-2 teaching in Malawi, Central Africa, and is currently working on a novel set there. Chief interest: Buddhism.

ROBERT A. CRAMPSEY was born in Glasgow in 1930. MA (Hons) History, 1951, ARCM, 1958, Brain of Britain (BBC) 1965, Churchill Fellow (USA) 1970. Author of *The Game for the Game's Sake* (History of Queen's Park Football Club) 1967, *Puerto Rico* (David and Charles Islands series). Radio and TV broadcaster and playwright. Presently Rector of St Ambrose High School, Coatbridge.

RICHARD FLETCHER was born in Lancashire in 1937. Graduated from Manchester University, 1959. Worked with a large manufacturing concern in Yorkshire before joining the lecturing staff of Glasgow University in 1962. Has written scientific papers and poetry as well as short stories, and has done some script-writing for BBC Schools Radio.

UNA FLETT was born in India but returned to this country as a small child. Has had several careers, including three years as a professional dancer with a French ballet company. More recent

189

ones include housewife, secretary, academic sociologist, civil servant and, currently, free-lance journalist with particular interest in the arts. The most continuous has been that of single parent to a daughter and a son now grown up. Has lived in Edinburgh for the last sixteen years.

JAMES SHAW GRANT is a native of Lewis and was editor of the *Stornoway Gazette* for more than thirty years. He wrote a number of plays for the Park Theatre, Glasgow and Pitlochry Festival Theatre, some of which have also been performed in Holland and America. He has only recently taken up the writing of short stories.

P. M. HUBBARD was born in 1910 and now lives in Galloway. Three of his four grandparents were Scottish. His staple output is suspense novels, but he also writes short stories, verse and non-fictional prose.

ALANNA KNIGHT lives in Aberdeen. Married, two sons. First novel published in 1969 as result of serial writing competition. Lecturer in creative writing for Workers' Educational Association, member of Scottish Arts Council's Writers in Schools. Short stories, ten novels including latest: *The Passionate Kindness* (on R. L. Stevenson), *A Drink for the Bridge* (on Tay Bridge disaster).

CARL MACDOUGALL holds the Creative Writing Fellowship at Dundee University and is Editor of *Words* magazine. He has written plays and published two story collections *A Cuckoo's Nest* and *A Scent of Water*. His work has also been published in a number of magazines here and abroad and broadcast frequently. He has worked extensively on creative writing projects through the Scottish Arts Council's Writers in Schools scheme and has written folksongs, of which the most famous is *Cod Liver Oil and Orange Juice*.

LORN MACINTYRE was born in Taynuilt, Argyllshire, in 1942. He entered the University of Stirling in 1967 without formal academic qualifications, and graduated in 1971 with first class honours in English. He has a Ph.D from the University of Glasgow for a thesis on *Sir Walter Scott and the Highlands*. In 1974 his first novel

Blood and the Moon was published in Inverness, and another in the same series is in preparation.

BERNARD MACLAVERTY was born in Belfast in 1942. Married with four children. Worked for ten years as a Medical Laboratory Technician. Went to Queen's University, Belfast to study English and is now teaching in Edinburgh. A collection *Secrets and other stories* was published last year by Blackstaff Press (Belfast). He has written and illustrated a book for children *A Man in Search of a Pet* which is shortly to be published.

ALAN MASON was born in Glasgow in 1954.

GRAHAM PETRIE is thirty-eight years old, born in Malaya of Scottish parents, educated at Dollar Academy, St Andrews, and Brasenose College, Oxford. He moved to Canada in 1964, and has taught at McMaster University, Hamilton, Ontario since then. He has published several short stories, film criticism in several magazines and a book, *The Cinema of François Truffaut*.

ALAN SPENCE is aged thirty and was born and raised in Glasgow. He was Fellow in Creative Writing at Glasgow University, 1975-7. His first book of stories, *Its Colours They Are Fine*, was published by Collins last year. He has also published a small book of haiku, *ah!* (1975). He and his wife run the Sri Chinmoy Meditation Centre in Edinburgh.

ANNE TURNER was born in Glasgow and educated at Whitehill School; now lives in Leeds where she works as a secretary. Her work has appeared in many periodicals and has been anthologized and broadcast.

ARTHUR YOUNG is the pen-name of a Scottish family doctor. Educated at Hamilton Academy and Glasgow University. Now practises in a New Town. Only lately came to serious writing.